CLUB MAFIA: THE CONTRACT

A DARK MAFIA ROMANCE

STELLA ANDREWS

Copyrighted Material
Copyright © Stella Andrews 2022
Stella Andrews has asserted her rights under the Copyright, Designs and Patents Act 1988 to be identified as the Author of this work.
This book is a work of fiction and except in the case of historical fact, any resemblance to actual persons, living or dead, is purely coincidental.
All rights reserved. No part of this book may be reproduced or transmitted in any form without written permission of the author, except by a reviewer who may quote brief passages for review purposes only.

18+ This book is for Adults only. If you are easily shocked and not a fan of sexual content then move away now.

18+

NEWSLETTER

Sign up to my newsletter and download a free book

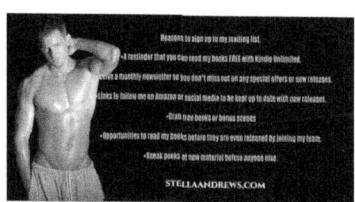

stellaandrews.com

CLUB MAFIA

They will save me; they will break me but not if I get there first.

Rockwell Academy
A place where the demons circle and destiny changes lives.
I was sent to join my twin.
Finish my education before fate reaches out and drags me in line.
Freedom is something I crave, but it will never be mine all the time I'm controlled by my father.
I don't have long – we don't have long because I'm not alone in this madness.

Five men walk beside me

Sons of the most powerful mafia families in the world.
The Boss - my twin who is my happiness dressed as a knight of hell and God help me if this is what comfort feels like.
The Demon - The man with a corrupt and twisted mind and dark soulless eyes that hold the secrets of Satan himself.
The Angel - A chaotic beauty of saint and sinner combined. Tall, broad, and devastatingly handsome. His hair color is the only light thing about him and the madness in his eyes would make anyone cower in fright.

The Savage - Brutally handsome in a twisted way, rough, capable and a machine with rippling muscles and close-cropped hair. Most women's dream and every man's nightmare. The strong, silent type.

Then there's The Beast – Strong, possessive, dominant. Loving, dark & delicious.

Demanding, sweet & protective. The one man I want but can never have.

One kiss will change history and one kiss is all it would take to ruin me forever.

I want **one night only** in his arms.
It will destroy us all.

Walk with the devil and he corrupts your soul and if you're very unlucky, he destroys it.

This is the prequel to Club Mafia. A dark & dangerous tale of stolen love. Rockwell Academy sets the scene and starts the reader on a dark and destructive journey of the most twisted kind. Lock up your daughters. The mafia is looking for an angel to sacrifice—it could be you.

High heat and scenes not for the fainthearted. If you love a dark Mafia romance, you're in the right place.

PROLOGUE
WINTER—AGED FOURTEEN

It's the waiting that's the hardest. Waiting for death because that's all we have to look forward to. It's always there, lurking in the shadows, ready to pounce at any second.

The woman's screams carry through the air on the breath of wind that dances around my face, and I shiver.

A strong hand reaches for mine and grasps it tightly and a deep voice whispers huskily, "It's ok, Winter."

Blinking, I try to distance myself from my reality and imagine a different life. A normal life where no demons lurk, plotting your demise. A life full of hope and dreams of happiness instead of a sense of destiny dealing you the death card.

The screams whip around us like the tainted souls of Hell, and I wonder how long she will fight. Last time it took hours for them to die. The wicked, the fool, and the damned. One dies and another takes its place. Business as usual in Hell.

Squeezing my eyes tightly shut, I try to picture a happier place. Anywhere but here would do, but all I can see is a void of black waiting for me to fall headfirst into it with no safety net.

My past, my future, and my present and if anything, I hope I don't have long.

It stops and I take my first breath.

Thank God she's gone.

If I feel anything, it's surprise that I feel no emotion. Did I really know her at all? A perfect stranger who only ever did one thing for me—give me life.

The soft sigh beside me makes me squeeze his hand a little tighter, and an arm wraps around my shoulders and a soft voice says, "I'll never let them hurt you, Winter. You have my word on that. It's just you and me now."

His words are meant to offer comfort, but they only bring a fresh wave of pain that stabs me on repeat most days because I only have him for as long as my father allows it. A lump forms in my throat along with the pain in my heart because what if...?

"Stop thinking." His voice is curt and dark, and I nod, beaten already.

"Angelo..."

"Listen to me, Winter." He interrupts me because we

both know I am the weaker one and he says roughly, "We will wait and when the time is right, I will set us both free. Trust me, I'm never going to let anyone hurt you."

Words fail me because how will that happen. We both know the hard life in front of us and we both know the sand timer is running fast and soon our lives will change forever.

We hear raised voices and Angelo sighs heavily.

"We should go before they remember we're here."

I don't want to leave but know I must, because locked in the treehouse with my twin is the only place I want to be in life.

Tomorrow, we will be separated. Two kids who will grow up fast because our fate is already decided. The thought of being apart from the only person I love in this world is too painful to contemplate, and I know I need to deal with what that means for both of us. I already know our story won't have a happy ending and if I'm sure of anything, it's that.

Some might think it strange that I don't cry for my mother. It was just a word, anyway. She was a stranger, a name and a blurred face of a woman who was supposed to do better and I just feel strangely detached from the whole situation and relief that she's gone. It's hard to admit, but my mother scared me and at least half of my problem is now solved. Her death was undoubtedly a painful one. A warning of what happens if you step out of line. A promise of a bitter end if you don't play your part in a family that doesn't know the meaning of the word.

Angelo pulls me up and I regard the bitterness in his eyes as he hisses. "I promise I will kill him one day."

That statement causes a brief smile to flicker across my

face and as his dark eyes bore into mine, we share a moment that blackens souls. Two halves of the same coin that will be separated physically, but our souls are joined forever. Brother and sister until death and my greatest wish is that I die first because without Angelo, I wouldn't want to live, anyway.

1

WINTER

Rockwell Academy

If anyone is surprised, I'm here, it's me. I never expected to be sent here, not in a million years. Life at Glendale Academy was ok, and I was happy to a point, but when the principal called me into her office and informed me that my father was moving me, I remember thinking he was calling me home. Apparently not. I'm to finish my education at Rockwell Academy and I have mixed feelings about that.

Principal Stoner smiles across his huge oak desk and I stare at a man who has seen it all before. He looks weary, a little beaten, and as if he's given up already.

He consults the screen on his computer and sighs.

"I've paired you up with Emma Bayliss. An excellent student who will guide you along the right path. She's one of our more studious pupils and an excellent role model."

Some may think it strange, but all I want is to blend into the shadows and keep my head down.

"Is she my roomie?"

He raises his eyes. "Yes, her previous one moved across state. I'm sure you'll get on; she keeps out of trouble, and I would be grateful if you followed her example."

The sharp edge to his words makes me smile because I'm guessing he's referring to my brother Angelo. This is his college, which is why I was surprised my father agreed to send me here and I'm not sure if I'm happy about that.

As much as I love my brother, it was good to have some independence from my family and try to pretend I was just an ordinary girl. For the most part, I succeeded, and I was happy enough, but there was that part of me that envied my fellow students because I will never have the opportunities they take for granted.

"Um, Principal. Stoner."

He looks up and I sigh.

"Is there any chance I can be scheduled out of my brother's classes? It's just…"

He looks at me with interest for the first time and I almost see pity in his eyes as he sighs, "You don't need to explain, Miss. Sontauro. I would feel the same in your position. You know…"

He shakes his head and says softly, "I'm always here if you need me. Failing that, Mrs. Grayson, your housemistress, will be more than happy to listen. You're not on your own; we can help."

I nod and yet we both know that nobody can help me, and my request was just to buy me a little time.

"Does he know I'm here?"

Once again, he sighs and rakes his fingers through his thinning hair. "I think he knows everything, Miss. Sontauro and I doubt I need to remind you of that."

A knock on the door makes me jump, and he calls out wearily, "Enter."

I look with interest at the girl who makes it through the door as if she's just run from a serial killer and I'm surprised to see the wild look in her eyes and the heaving of her chest. Her eyes are wide, and she looks scared shitless, and I catch the principal's eye, noting he looks defeated already.

"Emma, is something wrong?"

"No, sir." She keeps her eyes on the ground and won't even look at me and he clears his throat and says with a voice filled with resignation.

"This is Winter, your new roommate. Show her around and make her welcome."

I smile, but she won't even look and an uneasy feeling washes over me. She knows who I am, which means I'm fucked before I've even started.

Standing, I head across the room and say gently, "Hi, I'm Winter. Thanks for helping me out."

She looks up and I see the fear in her eyes, which makes me sad. Smiling, I try to set her at ease, and she nods, the curiosity edging her fear slightly away.

"You may go."

The principal's voice makes her jump, and she looks toward the door as if there's a firing squad waiting outside.

Taking matters into my own hand, I turn the handle and as I step outside, my heart sinks.

For fuck's sake.

Now I know why she was so scared because filling the hall with dark rage is the one person I hoped to avoid for a few hours at least.

He's not alone.

Four guys stand with him and it's difficult to breathe the toxic air that surrounds them. Full of menace and wearing a dark edge like a uniform, these men in waiting would scare the devil himself.

I can't even register them though because leaning against the wall, watching me approach, is Angelo and by the looks of things, he's not that happy to see me.

"Winter."

"Angelo."

Emma is silent behind me, and I know she's trying not to breathe for fear of attracting their attention and I sigh heavily and make my way toward my twin and whisper, "Thanks for the welcoming committee but you're scaring the pants off my new roomie."

The flash of his eyes and the dark twisted grin makes me smile and before I know it, his arms reach out and pull me close and as they wrap around me, it feels a lot like home.

Resting my cheek on his chest, I breathe in the familiar scent and as he kisses the top of my head, I can almost believe I'm happy. Angelo is happiness to me dressed as a knight of hell and God help me if this is what comfort feels like.

He pulls back and says in his low husky voice, "We'll talk at the house."

"No!"

"No?"

I sigh with exasperation. "I'm going with Emma, and you are going to let me. This is my last shot at freedom so give me that at least. I just want you to stay away and let me be normal for once."

He doesn't seem shocked and my heart sighs with relief when he takes a small step back.

"If that's what you want."

"It is."

I stare at him defiantly and he nods. "I'll be here if you need me."

He looks past me and the amusement in his eyes makes me turn to watch the strangest scene.

One of his friends is watching Emma like a wolf salivating after his next meal, and she is finding the whole experience extremely unnerving. I'm not surprised because this guy looks as if he's just escaped from an institution and the slightly mad look in his eye complements a chaotic beauty of saint and sinner combined. Tall, broad and devastatingly handsome, his hair color is the only light thing about him and the mad eyes that stare at my new friend would make anyone cower in fright.

I look at Angelo in disbelief and he smirks before saying abruptly, "We're leaving."

Without another word, he heads away down the hall and his friends just shrug and follow him without another look in our direction.

Immediately the atmosphere lightens, and I wonder if I need to resuscitate my guide because she slumps against the wall and takes in deep breaths of air.

"Are you ok?"

I feel quite concerned, and she shakes her head.

"That was intense."

"Not really." I roll my eyes. "Just ignore them. It works for me."

She looks shocked and says with a quiver in her voice, "Angelo's your brother?"

"Yes. Twin brother, actually."

"I'm so fucked."

"Why?" I can't help but laugh and she straightens up and looks around as if the walls have ears. "With due respect, Winter, your brother is not the kind of company I keep. They wouldn't want my company anyway, but I try to stay invisible around that group of guys. Most people do unless you've got a death wish or like to dance with the bad boys. When I say dance, I don't mean actually dance, I mean..."

She takes another deep breath and laughs nervously, "Sorry, I'm rambling. You'll figure it out soon enough, but just for the record, they scare the shit out of me, just saying."

We start walking and I do a little digging. "How does it work around here?"

"Same as most schools I guess, but there's a big difference where it concerns your brother and his gang."

"I kind of expected that, but aside from them, what's it like?"

For the first time, she smiles. "It's good mainly. The teachers are ok and the facilities the best in the State. If you like sport, you're in the best place and academically it sends more students to the ivy league than most others."

"What are you studying?"

"Law."

She turns and I note the light in her eyes as she says with excitement, "I'm trying for a place at Harvard. I study a lot, so you'll have to excuse me that. Though if you like to party, the best ones are at the Augustus house."

"Why are they the best?"

"Because of the guys who throw them. I mean, seriously

loaded, super good looking and they throw the best parties. Not that I'd know about that first-hand of course, but if that's what you're looking for, try to get friendly with the cheerleaders. They're regulars there and could get you a pass."

"I'm hardly the cheerleading type."

I laugh softly and she shakes her head. "Maybe not, but you are *their* type. In fact, I'm guessing you're most guys type, some girls too, not that I'm a ... well, I like guys, not that any like me that is, but you know what I mean."

She looks so awkward rattling words around like confetti as her nerves get the better of her and I rest my hand on her arm and smile. "Just for the record, I know exactly what you mean. To be honest, I'm not one to party much myself and like to study too. Maybe we can be study buddies."

She looks a little shocked.

"Really."

"Yes. I would like that."

She smiles, but I see she doesn't really believe I'm genuine, which saddens me a little.

Emma is the typical nerd that gets bullied at most schools. Practical clothes with oversized sweaters and jeans. Her brown hair probably always tied in a messy ponytail and her huge thick glasses making her eyes look larger through the lenses. Her acne is out of control and there is not a scrap of make-up on her face. She's also larger than average and obviously prefers to study rather than exercise and I feel bad for her because she obviously has low self-esteem because of years of being ignored.

As we walk to our dorm, I think about Emma. The fact one of Angelo's friends was giving her unwanted attention makes me mad. He was playing with her. Making her feel uncomfortable and I am not happy about that at all.

Thinking of my brother gives me mixed feelings. On the one hand, I'm happy he's here. I missed him so much but know we are better apart. He has grown into the dark madness that lies inside his soul, and I am doing my best to detach myself from mine. We need each other but need to be apart to survive and once again, I wonder what my father's plan was in sending me here at all.

2

ANGELO

It hurts so much. Just seeing her here reminds me the clock is ticking and I'm no further forward with an escape plan.

"So, that's Winter."

I look sharply across at Malik, who is studying me with a thoughtful expression.

"Keep away from her."

I stare at my friends through dark eyes. "Nobody goes near my sister, final word. Look *out* for her but don't look *at* her. There's a difference."

Malik nods. "What's your plan?"

I lean back on the couch and sigh. "We make her time here count because knowing my father, he has a particular future already mapped out for her."

"Bastard." Alessandro heaves his huge frame into the seat opposite.

"They're all bastards."

I nod. "We all have that in common."

There was a reason we gravitated toward one another,

and it has everything to do with our families. Mafia. Each one of the five of us have a connection with the dark side and sharing a house in our college years seemed like one big fuck you to the establishment. Rival families in the real world outside Rockwell Academy, but inside we are tight like brothers. Our families hate our friendship but considering we all hate the fuck out of them, there is nothing they can do about it.

Malik tosses me a beer from the fridge.

"Is she invited tonight?"

"You heard me. Stay away from Winter."

I sigh because the last place I want my sister is at one of our fucked-up parties.

I look across the room at Flynn, who is casually messing around with a hunting knife.

"Stay away from her roomie, too."

He looks up and dark eyes meet mine and just for a moment of madness, we are locked in a battle of wills. I watch as his eyes narrow and his expression darkens and then his husky voice heads my way with a soft, "I'll consider your request."

Ivan snorts as I roll my eyes. "God help me, why did fate deal me this fucked-up friendship group?"

Ivan drops into the seat beside me and pushes me playfully. "Because we're all we've got."

"And Winter." Leaning forward, I regard my friends through hooded eyes and hiss, "Treat her like your own sister and keep it that way. She has one year left of a normal life; hell, we all do, so let's make it count. Keep your eyes on her but touch her and I'll kill you. Nobody messes with Winter, understand."

I stare at them with a promise in my eyes and as they

nod in turn, I breathe a sigh of relief. Winter being here is a complication I could do without, which is why I'm guessing my bastard father sent her here. To mess with my head and distract my attention from the fact I'm about to graduate into a lifetime of hell and he is one unforgiving devil who wouldn't know what family meant if it was shoved up his fat ass.

"What's the plan tonight?"

Alessandro yawns and looks bored already, and I shrug. "Usual bitches and wannabees. I'm guessing three hours tops before the fun really starts."

Ivan snorts. "As if you can wait that long. What's it tonight?"

"Maybe poker. We need to brush up our skills in that direction."

"Who did you invite?"

Ivan looks interested as I smirk. "Joey and his gang of fuck boys."

"So that means..."

I nod. "They'll be followed by most of the bitches that like the idea of a bad boy between their legs."

Flynn yawns. "I may pass. Those girls have more STDs than I'm happy with."

"You take the door then."

Malik's smooth, dark voice heads across the room. "This should be easy."

I nod, anticipating an evening where we screw with more than their girls. Our poker nights are legendary, and I'm feeling particularly antsy tonight.

Sighing, I look at my watch. "We've missed first period. Best show up to the next. It's Miss. English."

I watch my friends heave themselves up and as we

head outside, I lock the door behind me. It's doubtful anyone would be foolish enough to try to break in, but some of the bastards who go to this school weren't blessed with a brain cell between them. I almost hope that one of them fucks up one day so I can deal with the rage that lives inside me 24/7 and only burns brighter each day that passes, closer to the one where my life falls off a dark cliff.

We head across campus as a pack and, as usual, nobody gets in our way. They know better and it's almost become boring, but as I watch the students scamper out of our way, dipping their heads and averting their eyes, I almost feel like picking a fight just for my own amusement.

Then a familiar face heads our way and a prickle of excitement runs through me as I say gruffly, "Baron."

He stops and nods, regarding me through the same bastard eyes that we all share.

"Angelo. I hear you're having a party tonight."

"Word travels fast."

He nods. "What's the theme?"

"Poker. You in?"

"Not sure. Maxim and the others are talking about heading into town."

"After then. It could be a late one."

"Usual stakes."

I nod, looking at him with interest. "Who do you have in mind?"

"Not sure, I'll think about it?" As he makes to leave, I stop him with a dark, "Make her familiar. No surprises."

He nods and heads off in the opposite direction and we watch him go thoughtfully.

"That bastard doesn't belong in that house."

Malik's low voice reminds me Baron is very different to us, outwardly at least. Inwardly, he's as corrupt as we are, and I know he will be there later with an angel to sacrifice, as always.

WE HEAD TO HISTORY, where the delectable Miss. English rules her class with the promise of a flirtatious look or a glimpse of her cleavage as she bends over your shoulder to study your work. Miss. English must only be a few years older than us and is one hot hazard that enjoys flirting with danger. Subsequently, her class is the most attended, and her results the best on campus because nobody wants to miss the pleasure that Miss. English brings to her lessons. Even the girls adore her. She is one of them, after all. Sweet on the outside but as corrupt as hell inside and I should know, because I've fucked her more times than I can count.

Ten minutes later, we are waiting patiently for her class to begin and there is not a spare seat in the room. As always, we sit at the back with me in the center surrounded by my faithful friends, and not one student looks in our direction.

Only a couple of braver cheerleaders look our way and blush when Ivan says gruffly, "You can touch, you know. Tonight, party, our house."

The longing looks they shoot him makes me smile inside because Ivan is like kryptonite to these women. Tall and broad with more muscles than Hercules, decorated in tribal ink that warns not to fuck with him. His dark features rarely smile and only his twisted grin indicates there's any emotion inside him at all. Girls fantasize about Ivan with his husky Russian accent and piercing blue eyes that promise a night of passion that is never repeated. Come to think of it, it's only Miss. English who gets that pleasure because one-night stands are the only thing we offer. Mind you, it would take a brave, or very foolish, woman to come back for more because we don't play by the rules, and it takes a certain kind of girl to tolerate that.

The door bangs opens, and Miss. English enters the room looking like a homecoming queen. Chief cheerleader and valedictorian all rolled into one and only the slightly wild look in her eyes tells me she's hiding a wicked wanton soul under that tight pink fluffy sweater, that's clinging to her tits for dear life. Knowing she prefers no underwear makes me shift awkwardly because fuck me, she is looking like every dark twisted thought in my head and as our eyes connect across the room, I watch her lick her bottom lip and pout in my direction and I know exactly what's coming.

As she gets to work, Malik laughs beside me. "Looks like your luck's in."

"It always is." I smirk because Miss English makes no secret of the fact she's hot for me and I'm not one to pass up a wild fuck in the stationery cupboard between classes.

Alessandro hisses, "Do you think she could handle two of us?"

"Definitely."

He laughs beside me and as I look at our provocative teacher, I wonder what she'll think when we both wait behind after class. It will be interesting to see what she does about that.

All through class, I picture what I'm going to do to her and when the bell rings, she looks up and says loudly, "Class dismissed."

The scraping of chairs almost drowns out her words as she says loudly, "Assignments due in three days. Oh, and Angelo, a word please."

My friends laugh as they head outside, and I nod to Alessandro to stay seated.

As the last student leaves, she looks at him and says in a slightly breathless voice, "Did you want something, Alessandro?"

"Yes."

He smirks and I stand and head toward the front and say huskily, "We need a private word."

The way her chest heaves and the excitement sparks in her eyes, tells me she's going all the way on this, and a small smile plays across her full lips as she nods toward the door in the corner of the room.

"Through there, we don't have long."

As we follow her through the door, I already know this will be quick. Sharing isn't really my thing, but I'm interested to see what Miss. English thinks about it, so as soon as we enter the small cupboard, I say roughly, "Spread your legs."

Her heightened color and small breathless gasp turns me on as she lifts her skirt and stands against the wall, her wet pussy glistening in front of me, and as Alessandro unzips his pants, I smirk.

"You ready, Miss. English?"

She nods, her breathing heavy and her chest heaving, and as Alessandro steps in front of her, I watch him roll on a condom and thrust inside. Her gasp is silenced by his large rough hand and as he pounds into her, I find it a total turn on. Stroking my shaft, I feel my own eagerness to join the party and as Alessandro clenches her ass with one hand and pushes in hard and deep, her muffled cry tells me she's just about hanging on.

He comes with a groan and as he pulls out, I'm straight in there, condom in place, as I finish what he started. Banging my teacher against the wall is one thing but watching someone else do it turns me on way more and as I come so hard, I place the palm of my hand across her face, pinning her to the wall. I don't want to see her face, I never do. It's just me jerking off inside a willing wet hole and that's all this will ever be.

As soon as we're finished, we toss the condoms in the trash and zip our pants, leaving our teacher with a smile on her pretty flushed face. There are no words necessary. We all know what this is, and Miss. English would rather die than admit what's been a thing for months now. This is all it is, and I doubt we're the only ones to enjoy the pleasure of her body, but it certainly makes history more fun.

"Fuck, that was good."

"I told you."

We head to our next lesson and for once, I'm feeling good about life. One year is all I need because when it passes, all our lives will change forever.

3

WINTER

Emma has been a very useful guide because she has shown me around, helped me with my schedule and taken me to my first lesson.

It was awkward heading into class for the first time and I felt the curious stares of the other students as I slid into a seat beside her at the front of the class. I know this will label me as a nerd, just being seen with her will do that, but I couldn't give a fuck anyway because I'm here to enjoy my freedom for as long as it's mine to keep.

We head out after the bell and Emma says sweetly, "I'll find you a locker. I think there's a few spare ones near mine."

As we head down the hallway, I feel the looks walk with me. Guys, girls and teachers all register I'm an unfamiliar face and I try to look unconcerned and friendly because the last thing I need is to draw attention to myself.

As Emma chatters beside me, I try to listen, but my mind wanders as I think how surreal this is. I could be normal. I could be forgiven for thinking I can have it all, but I know as soon as I graduate, I will be married off as part of a trade deal with a rival family. The men get to continue the family business and the women marry into power. It's always been that way and just thinking of that fate waiting for me makes me want to run and never look back. I want to make my own choices, make my own plans and live a life free from anger and pain. I'm a fool if I think that will ever happen, but Angelo has told me he will protect me or try to at least.

Emma stops in front of a bank of lockers and says with a hint of excitement. "Here it is. Fallon Edwards moved on last week and I knew it was going spare."

She opens the door, and we hear a low drawl. "What have we here?"

Her wide eyes look at me from behind the door and I look with interest at the person who spoke. I see a large, buffed guy wearing a jock sweater, and it's pretty obvious he's one of the football team and from the look of the girl holding onto his arm, she's a cheerleader. She has the most beautiful blonde hair and brown eyes that are regarding me with a malevolent gleam in them and before I know what's happening, the guy slams my locker door shut, hitting Emma's face so hard I think I hear her bones crack. Her grunt of pain makes my blood run hot and I say loudly, "What the fuck…"

That's all I manage to say because suddenly, out of nowhere, a guy appears who makes my blood run cold because for the second time today, I stare into eyes dancing with madness. I watch in disbelief as he slams the jock's face into his own opened locker and continues smashing it with a look of fury on his face. He doesn't stop and the screams of the cheerleader does nothing to deter him and as he smashes the guy's face to pieces, time stands frozen in a moment of pure terror. Still holding onto the flaying guy, he hisses, "Get her to the medical room."

Jumping to attention, I see Emma with a bloodied nose, trying desperately to stem the blood flow with tears pouring down her face. Taking her arm, the last thing I hear is him saying roughly, "Fuck off, bitch."

The sound of the girl running down the hall is almost hidden by the constant thud as her boyfriend's face hits the back of his locker on repeat.

Emma is crying and I am running on disbelief because I have never witnessed anything like that, and I've seen some fucked up shit in my time. I never expected that, though, definitely not from him.

Despite the fact she's completely traumatized, Emma guides me to the medical room and, as we step inside, the nurse looks up in disbelief. "What happened?"

"She fell."

I squeeze Emma's arm in a warning and Emma sniffs. "I'm such a klutz."

I can tell the nurse doesn't believe a word of it and as she takes charge of my friend, I shrink under the disapproving sneer from her pinched lips.

I have no choice but to sit and wait and as I think about what happened, I still can't understand why. It made no sense. Why would the guy pick on Emma like that and where the fuck did Angelo's friend come from?

Picturing the dark fury on his face and the wild look in his eye, my soul shivers. There's something beautiful about that guy. Malevolent stormy eyes disguised by beauty. Long dark lashes hide many secrets within them, and the slightly lost look of a psychopath makes my soul weep. The bleached blonde hair that makes him look like a fallen angel and the troubled aura that surrounds him makes him appear almost demonic disguised as an angel.

Emma is soon back and looks as if she's fought a war. If anything, I'm surprised the jock hasn't made it here already and I'm keen to get away before he does.

Taking Emma's arm, I help her out and she whispers, "I can't believe that just happened."

"Neither can I." I look at her sympathetically. "Do you want to go back to our room and have a lie down? I can fetch anything you need."

She sniffs and winces as her injuries introduce themselves. "I've got math. I can't miss a lesson."

"But…" I stare in disbelief as she says almost ferociously, "I *won't* miss a lesson. I've worked too hard to let something like this set me back."

As we walk, I feel a little lost because I haven't got a clue what's happening here and as Emma strides off with determination, I can't do anything else but follow her.

She stops outside a classroom and says wearily, "You're in here. I'm next door, so I'll wait for you when the bell rings and we can grab some lunch and I'll head back and fix this."

She doesn't even look at me as she heads off and I can't help but feel the despair growing inside me. Day one and I'm already caught up in some serious shit, despite everything.

As I head into the room, I see the teacher look impatiently at his watch.

"You are?"

"Um, Winter, sir."

He consults his list and nods, and only the slight nervous tic in his jaw reveals he knows exactly who I am.

"Take any spare seat."

Trying not to catch anyone's eye, I take the nearest one and stare blankly in front of me.

I can feel the eyes on my back, though. There's an atmosphere of danger, curiosity and fear surrounding me, and I wonder if they know already, or if it's just my overactive imagination playing tricks on me.

As I concentrate on the lesson, I'm pleased to find I'm familiar with the work. In fact, I'm pretty sure we did this last semester, so at least I'll have an easy ride for a while. I try to shut out what happened before and I almost manage it, but as the bell rings and the class is dismissed, someone stops by my desk as I make to stand, pushing me back down in the seat.

Looking up, I see a girl sneering at me who is almost a carbon copy of the cheerleader from earlier. Then I see the girl herself, hovering behind her friend, looking nervous as the first girl hisses, "Watch your back, nerd. Tell your little friend nobody makes a fool of us. My friend will need surgery for the mess that bastard made of his face, and we are holding you and your idiot friend responsible. So, watch your back because your face will soon be unrecognizable when we've finished with you both."

Sighing, I look up into a face twisted in animosity and say in a low voice, "Back off. You don't intimidate me. I've dealt with worse, so run along and shake your pom-poms somewhere else. Don't play with the dark side unless you can deal with the consequences of that."

She just straightens and laughs in my face.

"So, you're a fool as well as a bitch. Well, bring it on

because you're about to learn who runs things around here and, like I said, watch your back."

She spins on her heel and heads off, closely followed by her friend, and I sigh. Day one, two enemies and a beating and it's not even lunch time yet. Just another day in paradise.

4

ANGELO

The place is filling up and I feel kind of excited for tonight. It's been a while since I felt any sort of excitement. I'm guessing that's a good sign at least.

Malik's low voice rumbles beside me. "I've got a good feeling about tonight. I'm feeling lucky."

"You always do." I chuckle and he shrugs.

"You make your own luck in life; if I've learned anything, it's that."

We watch a couple of girls stride confidently inside and scan the room as if looking for someone–or something. Their eyes lock on Ivan, who is sitting on the couch looking bored already, his feet on the table, downing a beer. They nudge one another and head his way and we watch with interest as they stop just short of him and hesitate. He looks up and I recognize the two cheerleaders from class and laugh to myself as they look at him with a fascinated hunger that he must be used to seeing by now.

He says nothing and just pats the empty seats beside him and as they sit one on either side, he says nothing and continues watching the game, almost as if they aren't even there.

"That's him for the night."

"You think?"

"Maybe not." Malik laughs and I relish the sound. It's as dark and twisted as his mind and, of all my friends, I think he's the most dangerous. Then again, there's Flynn, of course. He's probably the most fucked-up individual outside of an institution, which is probably why it's best he remains in the shadows, making sure the right people get a foot through that door.

Our parties are legendary on campus. If you want a night of darkness, no boundaries and a walk on the dark side, then step inside. Even girls like the wholesome-looking cheerleaders are curious and some even come back. What can I say? We offer a service second to none. Walk with the devil and he corrupts your soul and if you're very unlucky, he destroys it.

"So, what's the plan?"

"We wait for the players to show and then the fun begins."

"Joey, I'm guessing. Why him?"

"He owes me."

"What for?"

"He had a problem with a guy hitting on his girl and doesn't want the shit that goes with retaliating. He's waiting on a call from a football rep and wants to keep his record clean."

Malik snorts. "Then he's fucked, because that guy is the dirtiest bastard I know."

Joey Zucker is the golden boy of the football team and tipped to go far. He's hoping for a spot on the NFL and came to me to deal with an unwanted problem that was causing him grief. Problem solved and now he owes me and if he loses tonight, his stake is really high because one night with his girl is the payment and I'm not sure if she knows about that yet.

We watch with interest as the man himself heads inside, closely followed by his girl and two of his friends. They don't usually attend our parties and I can taste their nerves from here. They form part of a different group who live next door. Baron's house where he lives with his three friends, Maxim, Duke and Gabriel. Seriously loaded and the most popular guys on campus, who throw the best parties and hang with the most attractive girls. Everyone wants in on their group, although there's still a morbid fascination with our den of sin that gets them calling on a regular basis.

Thinking of Baron, I wonder why he's there at all. Seriously twisted and definitely more one of us than them, he can't help himself and often heads our way for an evening of corrupt pleasure. I'm in no doubt he'll be here later. He just can't keep away and outside of my own friends, he's the only person I can stand being in the company of.

"Prepare yourself." Malik laughs and I see Eden heading my way and feel a prickle of irritation at the sultry look on her face. She has her sights set on me and has tried every trick in the book to grab my attention. We hooked up once and she thinks that buys her my promise ring, and she has tried everything since to make me her guy. She thinks intimidating others and proving she's the meanest girl on campus will cut it and as she saunters across in her slutty low-cut top and short skirt, she already thinks she's got this one in the bag.

Malik whispers, "Do you want me to distract her?"

Thinking of his idea of a distraction, it would almost be amusing to say yes, but I feel like kicking her into touch myself and say with an ominous edge to my voice, "No need, this won't take long."

"Mind if I watch."

"Be my guest."

She reaches me and smiles with a look of longing that many would adore. Not me. It's not the same if they want me. I'm not into relationships and it's the chase I love. The hunter stalking his prey and going in for the kill. That's far more pleasurable and having it presented to you on repeat most nights just gets boring over time.

"Eden."

"Angelo."

She pouts seductively. "You're looking good."

Malik snorts beside me, and I twist my lips into a smile and nod. "Thanks."

She looks around the room and says softly, "It's getting crowded in here. Do you fancy going somewhere we can um, talk?"

"No." I shrug and sip my beer, loving the insecurity in her eyes as she tries to claim my attention.

She glances nervously at Malik and then grabs some courage from deep inside and moves a little closer. "You know, we could be good together."

"We already were." I shrug and she takes that as a sign of encouragement and smiles, almost with relief. "I thought so too. Do you fancy keeping me company tonight?"

"No."

The look of anger on her face is quickly shown the door as she tries to disguise the hurt in her eyes and she whispers, "Why not?"

I shrug. "Because you just aren't good enough, Eden. Go and try your luck with someone else. I'm not interested."

"You were the other night, very much so if I remember. In fact, you were interested three times over."

Malik laughs out loud, and she looks at him with anger. "Did I say something funny?"

Malik tenses beside me and I watch with interest as he leans closer and hisses, "Watch your mouth and step away. You're no longer required. Go and find someone else to play with, because, as the man said, you're just not good enough."

I must admire her spirit because she stands her ground and faces me with defiance flashing from her green eyes. "Is that what you want, Angelo? Do you want me to find someone else to play with because it wouldn't be hard?"

"I think I've made my position clear, Eden. Run along and enjoy your evening. Remember to use protection. I'd hate the guy to end up at the clinic after."

"You bastard."

She looks on the verge of a breakdown and I take great comfort in that and as she turns away, I watch her stumble across the room with none of the confidence of earlier.

"That told her."

Malik sounds as if he enjoyed the show and I shake my head. "For tonight, anyway. She'll be back."

"You bastard.' Malik laughs again because we both know if I looked at her in a certain way, she would forgive me in a heartbeat and, to be honest, this is getting old. Being bad comes as naturally to me as breathing and I'm weary of it. There are no challenges here. No reasons to try, which is why I invented my poker nights. It makes life a lot more interesting and as Joey heads my way with his pretty girl in hand, I feel my interest stirring because Claudia Woodley is the prettiest girl I have ever seen and looks as nervous as hell as we watch them approach.

"Hey, man." Joey slings his arm around her shoulders and pulls her in close, almost as if that ensures her safety.

"You up for the game later."

"Are you?" I stare at his girl pointedly and I love how his skin pales under the light, and he licks his lips. "I'd kind of hoped..."

"Non-negotiable." I'm quick to cut him off because he knew the terms of our contract and that was his angel to sacrifice as payment. I remove the threat to his squeaky-clean image, and he pays me in kind. I don't need money and there's definitely nothing else he has to offer, and I love watching him nod in defeat as he realizes he has no other choice.

I wonder if he's warned Claudia about the night she could end up having, and I'm guessing he hasn't. Just the innocence in her eyes as she stares at us with fascination tells me that and I'm loving the feeling of power it gives me, knowing that I can't lose on this. Joey is good at football but lousy at poker which is why tonight will be more enjoyable than most when I watch the defeat on his face with every card exposed, pushing him further toward the realization that his girl may well be another's by the morning. Not that I keep them, but it's doubtful she will go back to him. They never do when they've been used as collateral to settle a debt of the most depraved kind. One night with me and she'll be ruined, mentally and physically, and I am keen to begin.

5

WINTER

Emma has retreated into her shell again after the attack and I feel bad for her. The rest of the day she tried to continue, but the curious stares of the other students drew attention to her, and she hates that. She likes to blend into the background and carry on with her day, but news of what happened earlier just won't go away and she is now the subject of gossip which makes her nervous.

At the end of the day, she shuts herself in our room and gets her head down, and no amount of persuasion can shift her.

I know she needs some time alone, so I find myself walking around campus unsure what to do next. Being new sucks because I don't even know where I'm going and so I decide to familiarize myself with the layout of the place and pop in my ear buds and start jogging.

The atmosphere is different here at night. Less busy and more relaxed. Groups hang around, laughing and drifting off to the various houses dotted around campus. I wonder which one I would have called home if I had been here for the duration, instead of the block usually reserved for freshmen where I have been placed with Emma who definitely doesn't qualify for a sorority house.

I pass the home of the cheerleaders and I smile at the white wood and pretty flowerpots positioned either side of the entrance. It looks a pleasant place to live but I already know I wouldn't fit in. I'm not like them and I never will be. Not far away is the one reserved for girls who like to challenge things. Clothes, gender and authority. These girls push boundaries and try to cause scandal and are forever organizing protests and causing disruption. They challenge the system and voice angry words at the establishment. I definitely wouldn't fit in there.

Jogging on, I pass the house where girls like Emma live, and I wonder why she never earned a place there. Studious and brilliant, these girls intend on breaking glass ceilings, which probably gives me my answer. They have a certain kind of confidence that Emma lacks, and they would be irritated by her nervous disposition and need to remain anonymous. Future CEOs and women of business, they wouldn't understand a girl like Emma, which makes me sad.

My attention is drawn to a house where the students appear to be flocking tonight. Set to the side, almost in the shadows and surrounded by darkness. Loud music is playing and I'm guessing there's a party there, judging by the number of students heading that way grasping handfuls of beer and a sense of anticipation as they head through the doors.

Suddenly, I see the mad friend of Angelo's, the one from earlier, watching a group head inside from his position on the veranda. Stretched out with a beer in hand, looking as excited as a kid who Santa missed. Feeling curious, I edge a little closer and as I hover nervously on the step, he says in a low husky drawl, "Turn and walk away, Winter. This is no place for you."

Rather than do as he says, I edge closer and stare into oblivion as his dark eyes mock me as he sips his beer with a flash of interest in his eyes.

"Thanks for earlier."

I don't know why I'm thanking him for messing up a guy's pretty face, but it feels like the right thing to do.

"You're welcome."

He nods toward the open ground in front of the house and says darkly, "I'd leave now if I were you."

"But you're not."

With one foot on the step, I look at him with curiosity burning deep inside and once again admire a beauty that would make a magnificent masterpiece.

"Why aren't you inside?"

"Maybe I like it outside more."

He appears almost human as he stares at me with interest. "He doesn't want you here."

My heart beats faster as he refers to my brother, and I nod. "I know."

"Yet here you are." He laughs softly and I edge a little closer. "He doesn't get to tell me shit."

This causes a smile to dance across his face, which takes my breath away. I could stare at him all night because this guy is seriously magnificent.

"Got one for me."

I nod toward his beer, and he shakes his head. "No."

"Water then, you'd save my life."

I grin and he leans forward, his forearms on his knees as he looks at me with a morbid curiosity. "You don't look in danger."

"Aren't I?" My voice is husky as I stare at trouble, and he leans back and grins.

"You already know that, so why ask?"

I've made it to the top step, and he just looks curious more than anything, and I nod toward the bench he's sitting on. "May I?"

"Probably not a good idea."

"You say it as if I care about that. Newsflash, I don't."

He shrugs and moves to the edge, allowing me space and as I sit, I feel as if I've won a battle many don't survive.

"Thanks again for earlier."

"How's your friend?"

His question surprises me because he doesn't seem the caring type. "She's ok, I guess. A little shaken, but she'll survive."

"Bastard."

I guess he's referring to the guy who slammed the locker in her face and I nod. "He is."

For a moment we sit in silence and then I ask, "Why did you help her?"

"I hate bullies." This makes me laugh out loud, and he cocks his brow. "Something amusing you, little sis."

"You. I'm guessing you could teach a bully how to perfect his or her craft. I hardly had you down as a knight in shining armor."

"What do you have me down as?"

He seems almost curious, and I say softly, "Someone who doesn't want to admit he has a heart."

"You think there's a heart in here?"

He pats his chest and laughs. "Empty, baby girl. There's nothing in there except darkness. Guess again."

"You like Emma. That's a start at least."

"I like nobody."

"Bullshit."

He laughs softly as I say with care. "I saw the way you looked at her outside the principal's office and you wouldn't come to her rescue if you didn't feel anything."

"If you want to believe that be my guest but you are so far from the truth, it amuses me."

"Then tell me."

A loud group of students approach and he says loudly, "Hey."

Their faces drop when they see him watching them and immediately the easy atmosphere darkens. He says huskily, "Fetch the lady some water, you have two minutes."

The group nod and push inside, almost with relief, and I laugh, "Does everyone do what you say?"

"Pretty much."

Almost immediately, a girl returns with a bottle of water and hands it to me with a shy smile loaded with curiosity. "Hi." She smiles and I return it. "Thanks."

"Go."

His curt voice sends her running, and I sigh. "That was rude."

"I don't care."

Grateful for the water, I chug it down and exhale with relief. "As I said, you're a lifesaver and I don't even know your name."

"Flynn, also known as The Angel."

This time, I laugh out loud. "By who?"

"Almost everyone."

"Why do they call you that?"

He shrugs. "Ask them. I couldn't give a fuck."

"So, Emma." I'm keen to dig a little deeper. "You like her."

"I don't."

He grins. "If anything, she fascinates me. A potential project to pass the time. Someone to coax out of her shell and watch burn before my eyes. Someone who never gets a chance to walk on the wild side and someone who would either break or manifest into a thing of great beauty because of what I can do. That is the interest I have in your friend, and it would be fleeting. One night only and then I lose interest. Never a repeat performance and that, my dearest Winter, is the *only* interest I have in your friend."

His words make me laugh and he looks curious. "Something amusing you?"

"Yes. Just the thought of Emma anywhere near you is so delicious it would be worth everything just to see the look on her face. You terrify her and I expect she'd die of a heart attack first. She just wouldn't survive."

"Then you issue an interesting challenge."

"I'm issuing nothing. Stay away from Emma. She has plans."

"Like what?"

"Harvard for one, and she doesn't need any distractions."

"One night only, Winter."

"That she may never recover from."

"That's the most interesting part of it. Watching how they deal with what happens."

"Why?"

"You know why." He looks at me sharply. "You live this

life, and you know how it works. We distract our minds just to survive. If I make one person feel good about themselves for the briefest moment, then I'm happy. Someone like Emma, someone who never catches a break."

I stare at him in surprise. "Then you are an angel."

"Your words, not mine."

Another group of students head up the steps and he calls out, "Turn around and walk away."

They stop as if frozen, and he says darkly, "Now."

They don't even challenge him and head into the shadows and I whisper, "Why did you do that?"

"Because they wouldn't survive."

"Survive what?"

"One of our parties. You see, Winter, some people are best off walking away for their own sanity. That group is vulnerable. Easily led and liable to do anything just to fit in. Corruptible and that, my dear, Winter ruins lives. They are best kept away for their own protection."

For some reason, his words bring tears to my eyes because now I see why they call him The Angel and I say in a whisper, "Then you do have a heart, Flynn. You just don't want to acknowledge it's there."

He settles back in his seat and drains the bottle before setting it down on the table by his side, where I notice at least six others. His eyes flash in the darkness as he says in a husky voice, "Conversation over. Go home before it gets darker."

I doubt he's referring to the sky and I shiver inside. Just thinking of the fucked-up games this guy probably enjoys makes me determined to keep Emma well away from him. I doubt she would survive being one of his projects and I kind of think he knows that which is why he told me what would happen if she went anywhere near him.

Standing, I nod my thanks and set the bottle next to his collection of empty ones.

"Thanks. For the water and the conversation."

He half smiles. "One time only, little sis."

As I jog on my way, I smile to myself. I like Flynn. There's something in him that touches a woman's soul and if anything, it makes me curious about his life outside Rockwell Academy. Maybe I'll ask Angelo one day, then again, maybe it's best I don't ever find out because I'm guessing his life is just as fucked as mine.

6

ANGELO

Joey is sweating–badly. We took the party to a private room and the only players are Alessandro and Malik, Joey and two of his friends. His friends were out long ago and Malik curses as his own hand folds, leaving Alessandro to laugh as he claims his win and says with satisfaction, "I'm out."

Joey looks nervous and his hands shake as he holds his cards, which show just how shit he is at poker. Then again, I knew that and as we place our bets, I say with an ominous edge to my voice, "Winner takes all."

He swallows hard and says nervously, "What. Already?"

I nod and he says helplessly, "Money, then, make this for money, not her."

"Are you breaking the terms of our contract, Joey?" I lean forward and my friends follow my lead and stare him down with looks that make grown men weep.

He swallows hard and says with a slight tremble in his voice. "No, of course not, it's just I thought…"

"Claudia is the payment I seek and nothing else."

His friends look around nervously because this is one fucked-up situation, and he nods in defeat. "Agreed."

The look of horror on his friend's faces almost makes me laugh because Joey has just proved what a sick fucker he is, and I doubt they will look up to him as much after tonight.

He lays down his cards and, as my own claim the hand, he whispers, "Fuck."

Alessandro laughs softly and Malik watches them all with the usual evil dark look he wears so well, and I say with satisfaction, "You have five minutes to bring her to me. My friends will see that you honor your bet."

Malik stands, closely followed by Alessandro and as Joey and his friends hastily leave the room, I stare at the hand of cards that brought me victory. It's always too easy. Guys like Joey fall into my trap on repeat and I wonder if I'll ever know what it feels like to lose.

I'm almost counting on it one day because at least then I'd *feel* something. Not this frozen existence that gets more fucked-up every hour that passes.

As always, when I'm alone, my thoughts turn to family, and I picture my father doing way worse than this. He likes to corrupt, harm and cause pain and that's on repeat most days. He wouldn't be feared as much if he wasn't, and I wonder if that's what it takes to survive this world. He certainly has a lot of enemies and very few friends, so I'm better off than he is in so many ways. I have four friends, five if you count Baron, and I have my sister. Now it's up to me to learn my craft well because I have always known I would kill my father and that day is fast approaching.

A tap on the door interrupts the dark thoughts I have of home and as it opens, Claudia enters, looking terrified. The door slams behind her and I know one of my friends will be guarding it and so I look at her with appreciation because this woman is worth every bit of admiration I'm throwing her way.

"You wanted to see me. Why?"

Her soft voice wafts across the room like silk on a breeze and I point to the chair opposite me.

"Take a seat. Do you drink whiskey?"

She shakes her head. "Not really."

"You may want to start now."

I pour her a glass and she looks nervous as hell. "Um, what did you want?"

Leaning back, I hold my own glass and look at her with a hooded gaze. "You."

The color drains from her face and she looks around as if there's a way to escape.

"What do you mean?"

This is the part I enjoy the most, the one where they learn their fate and I say almost as if bored, "Joey offered you up as payment for losing so we can do this the easy way, or the hard way, your choice."

The glass stops mid-air, and she stares at me with a stunned expression. "You had better be kidding me."

Leaning forward, I fix her with a dark look. "I'm not."

"No." she says angrily, and I shrug. "Your call. I never force myself on a girl; not my thing."

She looks relieved and her shoulders relax a little. "That's it, I get to leave."

"If you like."

She stands and I say darkly, "Tell Joey the bets off and he can say goodbye to his career."

"What did you say?"

I shrug. "I did him a favor; you a favor, actually. Remember the guy who attacked you at the club in town. Drugged your drink and tried to force himself on you."

She sits back down.

"Remember the reports of what happened to him the next day."

"You?"

I nod, setting my glass down. "Joey came to me with revenge in his heart. He asked for my help, and I removed your problem from society and protected your boyfriend's image. He gambled away his debt and a night with you was the payment." I laugh softly. "To his credit, he tried to change my mind and offered me money instead. I think he really likes you and would have offered me anything to save you this, shall we say, degrading situation. But in my world, a bet is a bet, and there is only one outcome if it's not honored. You walk away and Joey's career goes down with him. Shame, really, he has a promising future."

Her eyes fill with tears and she whispers, "So, either way, I get fucked by a bastard."

"That's life, baby. Just be more careful about the company you keep in the future."

She looks down and nods. "I have no choice then."

Leaning across the table, I grab her chin and force her to look at me, relishing the hurt in her baby blue eyes. Strumming my finger across her lips, I whisper, "Like I said, you can do this the easy way or the hard way. You see, if I were in your shoes right now, I would be mighty pissed at my so-called boyfriend. He has gambled with you and that can't be a great feeling. What better revenge than to enjoy the fuck of your life and walk away with your head held high. One night only with no strings attached. A night of passion with no regret in the morning. A walk on the wild side that will leave you feeling empowered. Don't be a victim, Claudia, be better than that."

"But it's not my choice."

"Are you sure about that? Say no and walk away with no regrets. This isn't your debt to pay, it's his. I wouldn't care. Either way, I take payment, but if you want to know what it feels like to take control and dance with the devil, now's your chance. I'm not a bastard. I'll make it a night to remember and…"

Pulling her toward me, I brush my lips against hers and whisper, "I'm guessing you will love every minute of it."

Pressing my lips against hers, I love how they eagerly part to let me in. Her soft moan of pleasure is all the encouragement I need as I kiss her slowly, tenderly even, and with one purpose in mind. Seduction.

As she presses in closer, I pull back and whisper, "One night only and remember, night is darkest the moment before the dawn, and I promise the dawn will be the first day of the rest of your life."

Her soft pants of desire give me my answer already and I say huskily, "Not here."

She nods. "Where?"

"Come with me."

Taking her hand, I lace our fingers together and as we walk into the crowd, I feel the curious stares follow us. We cross the room and make for the staircase, and I laugh to myself when I see no sign of Joey or his friends. Eden catches my eye and I smirk as I lead Claudia up the wooden staircase and the look she shoots her makes me wonder if Claudia will be ok. Eden has a particularly evil streak in her that probably involves an attack of some kind, so I'd be wise to offer Claudia my protection after this. I'm not a bastard, not really. Just a fucked-up individual who gets his kicks this way.

As I lead my prize to my bedroom, I feel good for once in my life because tonight is all about giving Claudia the night of her life with no regrets in the morning and I'm guessing Joey will be looking for a new girl on his arm when his old one wakes up in mine.

7

WINTER

It takes a week before I settle in and finally begin to feel at home at Rockwell Academy. Most of the time it's ok, just the usual shit to deal with being the new girl brings, but for the most part Angelo keeps away and I doubt anyone knows our connection outside of our own friends. Not that I have many, just Emma, because being paired up with her has earned me a ticket to oblivion, but I'm cool with that.

Occasionally I catch the eye of someone. The cute guy in english who sits behind me, the confident one in science and the girl who apparently hated me on sight in math but I'm happy to stay as I am. Emma, as it turns out, is great company. Once she got past her nerves, she relaxed, and I love her wicked sense of humor and ability to sum up a person in a couple of words, making me struggle to keep the laughter in.

I suppose that's what gave me courage when I turned the corner on my way to class and saw two girls beating the shit out of another one in the stairwell.

"Hey!"

I drop my bag and head toward them and one of the girls' shouts, "Keep out, this is none of your business."

"You reckon." I race to help and come up against the first girl who shoves me roughly back. The sound of the other girl grunting in pain spurs me on as her head slams back against the concrete wall and I see the fear in her eyes.

Swinging my arm back, I crack my fist against the face of the girl holding me and she cries out in pain as I make contact, causing her friend to stop for a moment and look my way.

"You stupid bitch."

She half turns which gives her captive a chance to land one of her own blows and as I wrap my arm around her neck and pull sharply back, her grunt of surprise is all I need to hear, and I jerk my arm back and slam her face into the nearby wall.

Then a strong hand pulls me back and I watch in shock as a huge beast grabs her by the throat and holds her against the wall, staring at her with a look of madness on his face and growls, "Back off, Eden and if you touch either one of them again, you're dead."

The tears are falling down her face as she gasps for air, and I notice her friend has left already and wonder if she's gone for help.

I can't look away as the beast holds her against the wall and snarls, "Now fuck off and never look at them again. We're watching you and if you want to survive the semester, keep your distance, you are no longer welcome at our place."

The tears fall down her face and as he releases her, she sobs, "Please, I'm sorry, don't cut me off."

He says nothing and just throws a cursory look at the battered girl shivering in disbelief and says with a grunt, "Go and tidy yourself up. Nothing happened here."

She nods, looking as shocked as I feel inside and looks past him and says in a shaky voice, "Thank you."

I nod, but that's all the time I have as the beast grabs hold of me and almost carries me away from the scene.

"Hey, what are you doing? Let me go."

He says nothing until we round the corner, and he pushes me into what appears to be an empty classroom and turns to face me with concern in his eyes.

"You ok?"

He rests his hand against my cheek and just seeing the concern in his eyes shocks me a little and, unused to acts of kindness, it does something to me inside. I hate the tears that start building and I brush them angrily away.

"I'm fine."

He just won't release me and stares deep into my eyes, and what I see reflected in his makes my soul weep and turn to sizzling ash. Those eyes hold the torment of a lifetime of hell in them and I know a lot of what that feels like and as he stares at me long and hard, something passes between us. Knowledge, understanding even and a sense of destiny weaving a magic spell because what I see in his eyes should have me running for cover and never look back. There's a warning mixed with a promise in them, and I just can't look away.

Neither it appears can he and we stand staring into madness together until the bell rings, breaking the surprising connection that joined us for the briefest of moments.

He drops his hand and pulls back, saying gruffly, "You should be ok now. I think she got the message."

"Who is she?"

I'm referring to the girl he warned off, and he appears to know that instinctively and sneers, "She's nobody. A mean girl who has her sights set on Angelo. He's not interested, and she decided to beat up his last bed buddy as a warning to them both."

"So, the other girl is Angelo's girlfriend." I'm surprised because I've never known him to have one and the beast laughs out loud. "I never said that. They hooked up for one night only, that's all they get."

"One night only. What is this? Have you guys signed some sort of secret pact or something?"

"What do you mean?"

"Flynn said the same the other night. One night only."

His eyes flash as he turns and looks at me sharply, "When did you see, Flynn?"

There is something like madness in his eyes as he stares at me long and hard, and I shift awkwardly on the spot. "The other night. I came to the house the night of the party and he wouldn't let me in."

"And." He looks angry and I don't know why, and it riles me a little.

"Not that it's any of your business, but we talked a little before he sent me away."

"I see." He looks thoughtful and then we hear footsteps heading our way and he sighs. "We should go. It won't look good if we're caught in here alone."

"Why not?"

He shakes his head and doesn't think my question

deserves an answer apparently and just heads off with no look back in my direction and I say quickly, "I never got your name."

"I never gave it."

He just leaves me standing and as the door swings shut behind him, I half smile. There was something about that guy that felt like home. Maybe it's because he's Angelo's friend. I recognized him from the hall on the first day and hanging out with him across campus. It figures I would feel at home with danger because that guy should have danger tattooed on his forehead because it rolls off him like radiation and is every bit as hazardous for my sanity.

Pushing the incident away, I head to math and feel uncomfortable when I see the girls from the hall glaring at me with malice. Throwing them a blank look, I sink into my seat and try to arrange my mind away from what happened and then, as the teacher enters the room, one of the girls slips me a note and I stare at the message in disbelief.

Watch your back. Nobody gets one over me

Sighing, I wonder if this girl is all there mentally because I'm pretty sure she must have a death wish or something and so I screw up the message and turn, throwing it sharply at her head with a look of derision on my face. The teacher shouts, "Miss. Sontauro, remain behind after class." I watch the blood drain from her face as she finally learns who the fuck I am, along with the rest of the class.

I take a moment to enjoy the dawn awakening, and as

the room falls silent and the fear creeps in, I relish my moment of notoriety, courtesy of my bloodline. Yes, Winter Sontauro is finally unmasked and I'm guessing will have a much easier ride from now on.

8

ANGELO

When Alessandro fills me in on what happened, I feel my blood boiling and it takes every ounce of restraint I have left in me to stop myself from heading to Winter and dragging her by my side. She was hurt, and it was because I gave her freedom with no protection and allowed somebody to get close to her.

Alessandro is watching my reaction and I know he is wondering what happens next. It's a madness we share. A hunger for violence, for retribution and for dishing out our own form of personal justice.

I keep my thoughts locked in my mad world for most of the time, but when it concerns my twin, it unleashes the monster within, and I know he is interested to see that side of me.

I almost can't breathe. It surrounds me like a poisonous gas, seeping into my bloodstream and corrupting my soul. Winter was hurt. Just one blow is enough to send me feral and even though I know my sister can handle herself, she shouldn't have to. Eden has overstepped the mark and it won't be pretty for her and so I say in a low voice, "Bring Winter to the house after class. We need to lay down the law."

I almost think Alessandro feeds off my anger because his eyes flash with excitement that is unusual. We don't get excited. Nothing challenges us here, and we are biding our time until we can unleash our anger on an unsuspecting world.

Even Miss. English can't distract me today and the fact I ignore her all lesson annoys her a little and as the bell rings she says sharply, "Angelo, a word."

The fact I stand and walk past her desk is one big 'go fuck yourself' and as I reach the hallway, my friends fall into step behind and beside me. Yes, we are closing ranks and they didn't need to be told. It's a sixth sense we have and now the mood has shifted because Winter was hurt.

Alessandro breaks away and heads in the opposite direction to bring my sister to me. I know better than to go myself because she wouldn't come if I carried her kicking and screaming. She won't be able to refuse Alessandro because that guy never takes no for an answer and his brute strength will be all it takes to carry her across campus against her will. I know Winter can fight, hell I taught her myself but only Ivan can match Alessandro in strength, which entertains us when we watch them practice on one another in the boxing ring we set up in one of the many empty rooms in our house.

We have named our house, The Edge of the Abyss, and it certainly feels like that. A holding cell ready to release the demons of Hell into the world. Ready to kill, maim and corrupt at the command of our fathers.

Every single one of us has our future mapped out already, and yet we have a different one in mind. Bonds and loyalties are formed at college, and I doubt any of our fathers saw this one coming. We may all come from different families on the outside world, but we belong to a stronger more united one now and when we leave the gates of Rockwell Academy, we do it as one solid unit that will be bound by more than just who created us.

"What's your plan?"

Malik falls into step beside me, and I say darkly, "We need to send a message and show people not to mess with my sister. I should have known this would happen and if I'm mad at anyone, it's myself."

"Do you think she'll be happy about that?"

"No." He laughs softly beside me, and I grin, the twisted one of a fucked-up mind and say darkly, "Clear out the top floor and make it fit for a princess. It's about time Winter fell into line."

"She's moving in." He sounds surprised, but he shouldn't. It was always going to happen because I can't operate knowing she is so close yet out of my sight. All the time she was at Glendale, I could breathe. Nobody knew us there. She had anonymity and was locked up in a girl's school, safe for now. Then my bastard father ruined everything and sent her here, the place where grudges run deep, and people's dreams of revenge are acted on. I have many enemies here, hell we all do and that's because we treat these people like dogs. They hate us yet crave the madness that surrounds us, and Winter is now involved in that.

Just picturing her caught up in a fight makes my blood boil. She could have been hurt–badly hurt, and she remains my only focus. The fact Eden messed up Claudia's face is no concern of mine. One night of pleasure has earned her a semester of trouble, and I couldn't give a fuck about that. She liked it enough when she wrapped her willing legs around me and pulled me in deep. She loved the consecutive orgasms I gave her and the night of pure pleasure. She wasn't complaining when she woke in my arms and I did it all over again, and even when I brought her pancakes and fed her myself, she didn't regret a thing.

To her credit, she walked away with her head held high, with none of the insecurities many have in the cold light of day. She even thanked me and for a moment I almost considered inviting her back that night, but our rule is there for a reason. No attachments and no baggage, except now I have one big problem, and that's keeping Winter safe.

We reach the house and as we head inside, I throw my bag on the couch and head straight to the kitchen and chug down a cold beer. Throwing one to each of my friends, we sit at the island and Malik sighs heavily. "We'll need to clean this place up. It's disgusting, the cleaners aren't due for two more days."

"Fuck that." Ivan growls, "Get someone in, I'm no maid."

For a moment we laugh because the thought of the huge, tattooed beast wielding a mop is an amusing one and Flynn grins. "I don't know. I quite fancy myself with a feather duster."

"Fucking pussy."

Ivan shoots him a taunting smile and Flynn shrugs. "Then again, I could tear its head off and stick the pole up your ass. Would you like that, big boy? I heard you like a bit of kink."

"Fuck, Flynn, are you looking to meet your maker or

something?" I shake my head as Ivan growls and Flynn just flips him the bird and a grin.

Malik, ever practical, says with interest, "How will it work and what happens when we party?"

"That's why she has the top floor. She can stay up there and keep out of it. There's a key to the door at the foot of the stairs. We lock her in."

"Man, she's gonna be pissed at you." Flynn shakes his head and I shrug.

"Couldn't give a fuck. Winter knows how these things operate. She will probably prefer it, knowing no horny fucker will be crashing her private space, which reminds me."

I throw them all a dark stare in turn. "Keep away from my sister. She's out of bounds."

Malik growls, "That goes without saying. You forget we know how this works."

"Just checking." I grab another beer and Ivan stands. "I've got a fight tonight; do you need me to stay?"

"No, go and play."

He nods. "I fucking need this. All this school shit is starting to mess with my mind."

As he heads off, I watch him go and feel a surge of pity for my angry friend. Of all of us, he finds education the hardest. He struggles academically yet has the most brilliant mind I know. Raised in Russia, he was brought here to live with the Bratva when his father was executed along with his mother. Ivan was taken as payment for their debts and molded into a killing machine. He cut up his first corpse, aged nine, and killed his first victim, aged seven. He has trained as an assassin of the most volatile kind and only boxing keeps his mind straight. He is the one that concerns me the most because without us to control and guide him, he's unstable and likely to explode.

We control Ivan to a point, but if he doesn't find an outlet for his anger, I'm not sure we can stop him from blowing Rockwell Academy to the moon.

9

WINTER

I'm surprised to find Angelo's friend waiting for me after class and as he lounges against the wall, the look he wears is one of troubled torment. For a split second, I see him first and my heart shifts as I sense a connection to him that I can't explain. Then he lifts those long lashes and stares at me with a dark gaze and I melt inside. Feeling angry about that, I scowl, and he straightens up and pushes off the wall. "You're coming with me."

"I've got study break, I need it." I toss my hair over my shoulder and make to pass, and a hand shoots out and grabs my wrist, anchoring me beside him as he starts walking.

"Hey."

I make to protest, and he says almost in amusement. "Save it. Nobody's listening, anyway."

He walks at speed, and I almost run to keep up and it gives me no time to think. I know this is my brother's doing. It's typical of him, sending his monkey in his place instead of having the balls to deliver the news personally.

We head outside and my rucksack falls off my shoulder, almost making it to the ground before he stops and sweeps it up and carries on, pulling me beside him.

"You don't have to walk so fast, you know. I'll come quietly. A little less pace, please."

He slows down and I catch my breath and now we're away from eager ears, I say quietly, "Thanks for earlier, that girl was seriously nuts."

"Did she give you any more trouble?"

I stop and stare at him in surprise. "You knew she was in my class?"

"I know everything, Winter."

"Fuck, you do." I laugh and love how his usually dark features twist into a grin, revealing a personality behind the brawn.

In fact, this guy is every fantasy I ever had, which is bad news for both of us and so I'm careful not to reveal how much he interests me.

"You never answered my question." He cocks his brow and I shrug. "A little. Usual stuff. The classic threatening letter that I tossed in her face, earning me a warning from Professor Adams."

He looks at me with a hard expression. "You got punished for something she did?"

"No, I got punished for throwing something at her head. He never asked why, and I never told him."

"I'll deal with her."

"You won't have to. The whole class now knows my heritage when he called me Miss Sontauro. I'm now officially untouchable."

He starts walking and I say casually, "You still haven't told me your name."

"No."

"Well."

"What does it matter?"

Sighing, I say scratchily, "Just tell me your fucking name, for god's sake. Is it something weird and embarrassing? I really hope it is."

He rolls his eyes. "Alessandro. Happy?"

He carries on and I smile to myself. Alessandro. Why does that name wrap me in comfort and make me feel safe?

We head toward their house, and I wonder what's going on. Knowing Angelo, he's pissed about something, probably something I've done, and I prepare myself for the battle that always happens when I'm around him.

As we near the house, I look at it in the daylight and note how clean it looks–tidy even. There's nothing out of place and the paint looks fresh and the windows clean.

"I'm impressed."

"Why?"

"The house looks so clean."

"We won't have it any other way. Flynn is a clean freak, and goes into a rage if anything's out of place and arranged for a team of cleaners to stop by most days. The rest of them are no different. It's the only thing we have any control over in a chaotic world. Surely you can relate to that."

This must be the longest sentence he's ever spoken, and I understand every word. We all live like this. Order is everything, and it appears to be no different outside of the fortress we usually live in. Angelo is the same, meticulously tidy, with an eye for the finer things in life. I'm just surprised to find his friends are the same.

"Who lives over there?"

I point to a similar house next door that also looks polished and orderly and he says, bored already, "Rich kids. Guys with more money than the federal reserves and more admired than the best influencer out there."

"They sound…" I falter and catch his eyes, noting the raised brow and interest in my next word. "Boring."

We share a look, and he laughs softly as I grin, and a moment of understanding passes between us. We are from the same mold–we all are, and normality may be something we crave, but it's also something we despise.

We head inside and Alessandro places my rucksack carefully on a hook by the door and says abruptly, "They're through here."

"They?"

He completely ignores me and strides in, expecting me to follow and with a sigh I fall in line because this needs dealing with and it's not going to be easy.

Angelo looks up as I enter a huge kitchen and I note he's surrounded by his friends, all looking at me with a hint of curiosity.

My eyes find Flynn and I offer him a shy smile, which doesn't go unnoticed by my brother as he says curtly, "Sit down, Winter."

He points to a vacant barstool.

Sighing, I do as he says because some battles aren't worth fighting and as I sit meekly waiting, he visibly exhales with relief.

"You were hurt."

"So."

He just throws me that look that tells me it hurts him

more than me to know it, and I feel my anxiety ebbing away. Being twins does bring with it a closer bond and if I thought anyone hurt him, I would be so angry I would hunt them down and make sure they could never hurt him again. So, I cut him some slack and smile sweetly. "I'm fine. In fact, now people know who I am, I'm sure those days are gone."

"How?"

"My professor. He called me Miss. Sontauro, that kind of let the cat out of the bag."

"I see."

Flynn slides a coffee toward me and winks. "You may need this."

"Thanks." We share a smile, and I can tell that irritates the hell out of Angelo because he throws Flynn a warning look that would cause a heart attack in any normal guy. Flynn just laughs and turns away and takes his seat and leans forward with interest, as if he's expecting a show of some kind.

"Why am I here, Angelo?" I feel suddenly weary with all the mind games, and he says tightly, "You're moving in."

"No, I'm not."

I stare at him with my stubborn streak firmly in control, and he shakes his head. "Non-negotiable. The top floor is yours and you can design it how you like. Just let me have the details and I'll arrange the makeover."

"No, Angelo."

He completely ignores me. "When we party, you stay in your rooms. Nobody gets to go there, not even us. Total privacy and your safe place. You will cook for us once a week and keep the place tidy. We have cleaners and a food delivery twice a week. Just add your requirements to the list."

"But..." I have no words and I'm beaten already, and Angelo knows that because he looks a little sad on my behalf and says gently, "It's for your own safety, Winter. I couldn't bear it if anything happened to you because of me."

"You think I got hit because of you?"

He nods. "I knew Eden would go after Claudia. I just never expected you to help out, which reminds me what a fool I am. You never could resist helping someone. It's not the first time and won't be the last. This way, the whole fucking campus will leave you alone, and that makes me happy."

I feel so trapped and despite trying to be strong, I feel the walls closing in on me and the tears build that I fail to disguise.

"But I want to be normal, Angelo." My voice sounds weak and troubled and from the look of torment in Angelo's eyes, I know I've hit him where it hurts the hardest.

He looks so tortured and shifts from his seat and heads my way, wrapping his arms around me and pulling me close. Just his sigh of relief and the tightness of his arms tells me how afraid he is for me. This isn't about Rockwell Academy and any threats that may bring. It's life. Angelo is afraid of what that will involve for both of us, and we are all we've got. Part of me understands why he's doing this. This is our time. However brief, it's a time when we can be together with nobody controlling us. The calm before the storm and as I sink into the familiar strong arms of my twin, I let my tears stain his shirt because, in truth, I wouldn't want to be anywhere else.

For a moment there's silence and then I hear him say roughly, "Get her friend's things too. She's moving with her."

Jerking back, I stare at him in horror, and he runs his thumb down my cheeks, wiping the tears away. "You won't be alone; you can have her. She'll keep you company; it's my one concession."

Glancing past him, Flynn throws me a twisted grin and I say quickly, "Emma will hate it. She'll die of a heart attack the minute she steps through those doors. She won't come and you can't make her. She needs to study; she wants to go to Harvard…"

He places his finger against my lips. "Quiet. She'll be safer here than anywhere."

"Are you sure about that?" I look past him to Flynn, who shrugs and grabs a beer from the fridge and Angelo says over his shoulder, "Hands off the girls, all of you."

He turns and says almost as an aside, "I don't think you've met my friends, Winter. Flynn is our psychotic friend who couldn't give a fuck about anything. You'll be lucky if he talks to you, otherwise he's like a shadow from your nightmares."

"Only yours." Flynn flips him the bird and Angelo sighs. "Ivan is the one with all the tattoos. If he likes you, he'll teach you how to curse in Russian. Failing that, he's only interested in fighting and fucking, so stay the hell away from him."

Ivan looks my way and nods as a sign of respect and, for some reason, a shiver passes through me. He looks so angry, battle hard already and I'm pretty sure those tattoos cover a world of abuse, judging by the dead look in his eyes. Brutally handsome, beautiful in a twisted way, rough, capable and a machine with rippling muscles and close-cropped hair. Most women's dream and every man's nightmare. The strong silent type by the looks of him.

"You've met Alessandro. Go to him if you need some heavy lifting or protection. He's a fighter like Ivan, but a little less brutal and won't bring the fucking homicide cops calling like our Russian friend here."

Ivan grins and Angelo sighs before pointing at a guy who scares the hell out of me just from his eyes alone. A killer's eyes hooded and unemotional, with dark Arabic features that hide emotion well.

"Malik is the brains in the room. Figuring out our enemies and planning their demise. He's the one to go to if you have a problem. He ensures the running of the place and makes sure we're all up to speed. Great with computers and responsible for security." I look at Malik and shiver inside. There's nothing there. Just anger and threats; a storm building that will involve heartache for someone down the line.

Angelo says. "Every single one of my friends comes from organized crime. Ivan is Bratva, Malik is middle east mafia, Alessandro Italian mafia and Flynn is west coast."

I look at them with a new level of respect and Angelo says darkly, "Take a good look, because this is your new family. I'm not talking about Rockwell Academy either, because when we leave here, we set up on our own."

"Angelo." I gasp and he nods, twisting my face to look into his emotionless eyes. "We have plans, Winter, and the first one is to set you free. Don't fear the future all the time you have us. Trust us, honor us and accept us because we are each other's future, and nobody is going to step in the way of that."

"But how?"

I want to believe him more than anything, but I'm not a fool and he will never win against our father and his whole fucked–up operation back home.

Angelo rests his head against mine and stares into my eyes, whispering softly, "We're taking them all down from within and we begin at home."

He strokes my hair like he would a favorite pet and as I see the person he has become it fills me with fear—for him.

10

ANGELO

It feels good having Winter where she belongs–with me. I can keep an eye on her and make sure she's happy—for now, at least.

I didn't like the secret looks she shared with Flynn, or the way Alessandro looked at her when he thought nobody was looking. I'll deal with them in my own way, but for now, we must settle her in.

"I'll come with you and help get your stuff."

She looks at me with a flash of anger in her eyes. "I don't need your help."

"I don't care. You're getting it, anyway."

Turning to my friends, I say quickly, "Malik, Ivan, I could use some help."

I stare at Flynn and Alessandro with a warning in my eyes and I can tell they note it because Flynn just smirks, and Alessandro looks resigned.

As we head off to the freshman block, Winter walks beside me, and Malik and Ivan walk behind us.

She sighs, "I need to speak to Emma. You must let me

go in first. She's going to freak out when I tell her what's happening."

"If you like." I'm bored already and could do without the added complication of her roomie, especially with Flynn in the same house and almost as if she can read my mind, she says urgently, "Keep Flynn away from Emma. What is it with him, anyway?"

"You tell me. You've shared cozy conversations already. Ask him yourself."

"Does that upset you, Angelo?"

There's a hint of humor in her voice, and I shrug. "Keep away from him. He's volatile."

"Aren't we all?" She sighs and I feel my heart ache for the childhood she never had. The weary way she speaks, and the lost look in her eyes. Winter deserves better than the life mapped out for her, which is the driving force behind my actions.

We reach her room and I hang back with my friends waiting in the shadows with a terse, "You have five minutes, then we're coming in."

She doesn't answer me and heads inside and Malik leans against the wall and laughs softly. "Oh, to be a fly on the wall. That girl will be scared shitless."

"I don't care. She's company for Winter, that's all."

"And Flynn?"

"Will stay away if he knows what's good for him. Nothing must ruin this friendship for Winter. She needs that girl more than anything right now."

"Then I'll leave it up to you to tell him because we all know Flynn works to his own agenda and wouldn't give a fuck if she was the Queen of England and he wanted to go there."

I watch a group of guys heading toward us and look with interest at Baron and his three friends. They stop a short distance away and Baron grins.

"Hey, it's not like you to hang around freshmen." He smirks, and I sigh.

"Just helping my sister relocate."

"Your sister, I heard something about that."

He smiles and I roll my eyes. "You fucking knew already, don't pretend otherwise. In fact, I'm guessing there's not a lot you don't know about, Baron."

His friends laugh and Max nods. "He's got your number."

I look at Max with curiosity because there is something about him that sets him apart from the rest. It's almost as if he's protected by them, and I'm not sure why. I know he has more money than anyone I know, and yet there is no knowledge of his parents, or where he even lives. His two other friends always flank him as if they're his bodyguards or something and I decide to dig a little deeper with Baron when he next comes calling. He always does, mainly in the early hours. Sometimes for cards, other times just to hang out, but when we're off the rails, he appears to like it more. Baron has a dark side that doesn't sit well with his friends and he could prove to be a valuable ally in the future.

"Do you need a hand?"

He nods toward the block, and I shake my head. "We're good thanks."

"Then we'll be off. We have a party tonight and should be there before the guests, at least."

They pass and as they move into the distance, Ivan says with interest, "They have the best-looking women at their parties. I may head there myself; I need some action tonight."

"Like you'd be welcome." Malik snorts. "You'd stick out like a bad smell."

"Then I'll head into town. I need something to take the edge off."

I look at him sharply. "What happened?"

Malik catches my eye and for the first time, I see Ivan has something on his mind that I've missed because I've been so preoccupied with Winter.

Ivan shakes his head. "Gregor wants me home; he's trying to arrange it."

"You never said, since when?"

"This morning, I got a text."

"Do you think he's messing with your head again?" Malik voices what we both suspect, because Gregor is always threatening to pull Ivan out of Rockwell. He hates his association with us, and I know he grills Ivan for information on our families and has told him to spy on us for him. Most of the time we feed him duff information for fun and Ivan takes great pleasure when his uncle fucks up at our hand. Malik is clever though, and it never looks as if Ivan was wrong, and it's become a game of cat and mouse we all enjoy.

Ivan sighs. "I think he's messing. It wouldn't make a difference to him either way. Most of the time, he's deep inside some whore at his club and the operation runs despite him. He's just an evil bastard who gets his kicks from tormenting others and I'm an easy target and I can't fucking wait to waste him."

Malik sighs. "Six months, that's all we've got. We had better step up and move things on."

A movement in the bushes catches our attention and Ivan moves quickly. Malik steps beside me and we watch as he pulls a trembling freshman out by his hair and pushes him against the wall.

"Are you spying on us?" Ivan leans in and sneers.

"No, I'm sorry, I promise."

For some reason, I believe him because this kid looks as if he's about to pee his pants and come to think of it, he doesn't appear to be wearing any.

Looking up, I watch a blind pulled shut and a window slam and I laugh, "Let him go."

Malik looks at me in surprise and I nod toward the floor above. Understanding dawns in his eyes, and Ivan laughs out loud. "I hope she was worth it."

The guy shivers as he clutches his pants and nods. "Fucking legend."

It makes us laugh and Malik says with interest, "Who was it?"

"Lauren Flowerday."

It's not a name we're familiar with and Ivan groans. "Even this kid's got lucky. I'm definitely getting laid tonight."

He releases the guy and nods toward the path. "Fuck off and don't go sneaking around listening in on conversations that don't concern you."

He almost runs off at speed and Malik laughs. "Maybe it's a good thing Winter's moving out if guys like that are sniffing around."

Just thinking of any guy near my sister throws a bucket of reality over me and I growl. "Five minutes are up. Follow me."

11

WINTER

Emma looks scared shitless and actually starts trembling. "Oh, please God, no, Winter, anything but that."

I try not to take it personally and sit on the bed and try to help her avoid a massive anxiety attack.

"It's fine. They'll keep away and have promised nobody will come upstairs, they wouldn't dare, and you'll get your own room, your own study even and all the food you can eat. Please say you'll come, Emma. I don't think I can do this on my own."

I can tell she's torn because the room we're in is so small there's barely room for her books and I say slyly, "Just think, Emma, your own desk, bookcase, and heaps of room to study. No worries and everything paid for. You can study without anyone disturbing you and you have the best security on campus. Please say you'll come, and the best thing is, nobody will give you any grief."

I know she's bullied by just about everyone in her classes and it makes me sad that just because she's studious and not bothered about fancy clothes or makeup, she's made to feel inferior. Emma is a beautiful girl inside and just isn't interested in the stuff most girls are.

She jumps as the door slams open, and Angelo stands there looking bored. "Times up, bring what you need, and I'll arrange the rest to be brought across in the morning."

I actually think Emma is going to cry because her eyes fill with tears, and she appears to be having trouble breathing. She can't even speak to protest and as Angelo steps aside and Ivan heads into the room, she inches closer to me as he says firmly, "Where's your bag?"

Quickly, I grab one and start filling it with Emma's stuff and thrust it at him, more to get him out of here than anything and as I do the same to Malik, Emma sits shivering on the bed as if zombies have entered the room.

Grabbing her hand, I pull her from the bed and as Angelo moves behind us, I swear I hear her whimper. I feel so bad for doing this, but I need her more than she needs me and if I can do anything for her, it's helping grab her some confidence from somewhere.

WE HEAD SILENTLY BACK to the house because any words of reassurance sound empty even to my own ears and it doesn't help that our escorts are surrounded by a dark force field. Sighing inside, I hope this is the right move because if I disrupt Emma's studies in any way, I will never forgive myself. It's important to me that one of us at least gets to live her dream and she is now my number one priority.

As we reach the house, I feel her fear and grasp her hand and squeeze it reassuringly.

"It will be ok, trust me."

As we head inside, Ivan and Malik head straight upstairs with our bags, and Flynn and Alessandro provide an unwelcome committee. For Emma, at least because she turns even whiter if that's possible the moment Flynn openly stares at her.

Flashing him a warning look, he shrugs and turns away, heading into the kitchen, giving us some much welcome space.

Alessandro appears to be brooding about something and doesn't look happy and I try to ignore him and concentrate on my friend, who is definitely in need of some form of help right now.

"This way."

Angelo is curt and to the point and yet I'm glad to follow him upstairs and see just what we've signed up for.

This house is huge, and I can't believe the number of rooms we pass with firmly closed doors.

"Are you sure it's just the five of you here?" I can't believe it is, but he nods. "This floor is where we sleep and there's a few other rooms spare for visitors, not that we have any, but they come in useful sometimes."

He doesn't offer any more explanations and I'm certainly not asking because I know what the spare rooms in our own home are used for and none of it is good.

We head up another flight of stairs and Angelo says gruffly, "This is your personal space. There's a door you can lock to keep others out and there are five rooms up here you can use how you like. Just tell me what you need, and I'll arrange it."

Emma is silent beside me, but I can tell she has relaxed

a little and as he turns to go, I say quickly, "You really didn't have to do this. I was fine before."

"We both know it was always going to happen, Winter. Just make the most of the next six months."

His words remind me what's at stake and the huge weight of sadness that has always lived inside me swells unbearably. Normality for six months and if this is what's considered normal, I've already started to fall into the abyss and this time I'm dragging an innocent angel in with me.

FINALLY, we're left alone, and I turn to Emma and say with concern. "Are you ok?"

She exhales and looks around with wide eyes. "I think so."

"Good. We should take a look around and decide what we need."

As we head through the rooms, most of them are fine as they are. Modern looking bedrooms with attached bathrooms.

"Which room do you want?" I give Emma the choice because it's the least I can do.

For the first time she looks enthusiastic, and I don't blame her because we could live up here with no worries and I'm already planning a way to make us self-sufficient.

"I'd love the one at the end that looks across the lake."

"Fine. I'll take the other one and we can use two as studies if you like, leaving one as a television room to relax."

"Sounds good to me." She sounds a lot brighter, and I say thoughtfully, "Maybe we should ask for a microwave and some kitchen facilities. I don't fancy those stairs just to make a snack. What do you think?"

She looks relieved as she nods. "That sounds amazing."

"I'll ask Angelo to arrange the rest of our stuff, but I'm pretty sure we can slum it here."

I grin and as she catches my eye, she laughs and the sound of it settles my heart. Thank God, it will be ok.

The next hour is spent unpacking and when Malik and Ivan drop the rest of our stuff off, it keeps us busy. Before long, we hear someone shout from the stairwell below, "Pizzas up."

Emma comes running, looking horrified. "Do we have to go down there?"

"I'll bring some up if you like."

"Please, I just don't think I'm ready to mix with them."

Smiling, I leave her to it and head downstairs and, as I wander into the kitchen, I swallow hard.

Ivan and Alessandro are standing by the fridge wearing nothing but sweatpants. and the sight of their toned bodies covered in ink makes me falter and my face burn when they catch sight of me. I am not used to this because nobody in our various houses ever ventured out in less than a well laundered shirt and, seeing the sweat glistening on their bodies as they chug down bottles of water, tells me they're fresh from a workout.

Ivan just slams the bottle down and growls, "I'm heading for the shower. Save some pizza for me."

He brushes past me and Alessandro smirks at the flushed look on my face as he heads my way. "You're gonna have to get used to this; just be grateful we're wearing pants."

He smirks as he brushes past my other side as Angelo

heads into the room, closely followed by Malik. The fact that Flynn is unaccounted for, and Emma is alone upstairs, causes me a moment of panic and I say fearfully, "Um, where's Flynn?"

Angelo shrugs, "Who knows, but the scent of pizza won't keep him hiding for long."

"Emma will be ok, promise me."

Malik laughs softly and they share an amused grin before Angelo sighs. "Your friend has nothing to fear from Flynn. He's got a few issues and if anything, he could help her. Just leave him and don't test him if you want a quiet life."

"What's that supposed to mean?"

I venture in and grab a box of pizza, intending to take it upstairs, and Angelo says abruptly, "We eat as a family."

"But..."

"As a family, Winter. Fetch your friend and tell her to wash her hands. You have five minutes."

Malik watches with interest as I snap, "Fuck you, Angelo. Neither of us asked to be brought here. Let us live the way we want to, even if it is under your supposed roof. Who made you the boss, anyway?"

Malik laughs out loud. "He is, actually. Your brother is the boss, and you've met the beast and the savage. Flynn is the angel and me..."

He grins darkly, "I'm the demon, so in this house, you play by our rules, or we make you–simple."

Angelo grins as I take a step back. "You wouldn't dare."

He shrugs. "I'd advise you not to test any of us because you don't know how things work around here. For your own sanity you will play by our rules because then you'll have an easy time. Test even one of my friends and I can't help you. We're a family and that counts for everything within these walls and if your friend can't wrap her head around that, I'll ask Flynn to teach her. So, run along and grab her hand and pull her in line right behind you because under this roof, you are controlled by us."

Tearing away, I run for the stairs, my heart thumping with anger. Bastards, every last one of them and now I'm here, I wish to God I wasn't.

12

ANGELO

I think Winter's friend may not last the night. As they sit at the table surrounded by menace, I don't think she's eaten one slice of pizza and it pisses me off. I can't stand fear, I never could, and she needs to deal with it before it destroys her.

Winter is pissed. I know that look in her eyes and won't say a fucking word even when spoken to. She's acting like a petulant child, and I'm embarrassed for her so I decide to teach them both a hard lesson because fuck me, I can seriously do without their shit right now.

The guys are antsy, probably because they haven't been laid in a few days and Ivan looks as if he's about to explode from boredom, so I say firmly, "Ivan, Malik, arrange a party for tonight."

They all look up. "But I thought..." Alessandro looks confused because I made it clear there would be no parties until the girls had settled in.

"I changed my mind." I stare at him long and hard, and he nods. "Fine, I'll get word out."

Flynn looks bored. "I'll take the door."

"Not this time."

I stare at Emma and love the way his eyes spark with interest as he gets the green light.

Winter looks worried. "Then we'll head to our rooms. We have study and…"

"You'll stay. It would rude not to because this is your welcome party."

"I don't want one." She pouts and I shrug.

"I don't care, you're getting one anyway and by the end of it you'll understand just how things work around here. This is your home, and you are about to learn what that involves."

"But…"

"Trust me, Winter, this is for your own good."

Emma looks terrified especially because Flynn appears to be undressing her with his eyes and Winter looks worried for her and stares at me pointedly, "You promised."

"That you'll both be safe. You will and if you have any complaints in the morning, bring them to me."

Ivan and Malik leave, and Alessandro looks thoughtful. "What's the plan?"

"No plan tonight. Just a party, plain and simple."

Alessandro nods and I know I've confused the hell out of my friends because I've already gone back on my word. The trouble is I feel bad. Bad for Winter and bad for her friend and they may not believe me, but this party is the best thing for them.

Winter sighs and as she stands I say quickly, "You can clean up and then get ready."

"Why us?" Winter looks pissed and her eyes flash as she suspects she's about to be made chief slave.

"Because you must help out and do your share. It may as well start now."

She pushes back her chair angrily and says roughly, "Come on Emma. The sooner we get this done the sooner we can get the hell out of here."

I smirk as they set to their task, and I nod to my friends to meet me outside.

We head around to the back of the house and as I light a cigarette, Alessandro growls, "I thought you quit."

"That was before my sister came to stay; maybe I didn't think this through."

Flynn laughs out loud. "Well, I'm feeling pretty good about that now."

"I thought you might."

Alessandro laughs softly, "Are you really unleashing Flynn on that scared shitless friend of your sister and can I watch?"

I nod, grinning as I imagine the sort of evening she's in for. "She'll thank me for it tomorrow, just be kind and remember who she is."

"Why wouldn't I be kind? She's perfect."

Turning to Alessandro, I fix him with a darker look. "That doesn't give you permission to spend time with my sister."

"Why do you say that?"

"I've seen the look in your eye when she's near you. Stay away, I will only warn you once."

For once he lowers his eyes, telling me my intuition was spot on. There's something between them already and it will be over my dead body, or Winter's more likely. Despite the freedom she's been given in her education, she has one job to do. Marry for power and make sure she's a virgin on her wedding night.

Just the thought of the man who my father probably has lined up makes my blood run cold. He won't care what sort of man he is, just what he can get out of the deal and my sister will be the one trapped in a marriage of fear. I need to make this time count for something, give her memories to see her through the dark days ahead and if I can allow her a little freedom, at least it will be under my watchful eye.

"I heard there's a party later."

We turn and see Baron standing nearby, leaning against a tree and I laugh. 'News travels fast. You in?"

"I might be."

"Only might."

"Depends on what the plan is."

"There is no plan, just a party."

He shakes his head. "I have those most nights, maybe I'll pass."

He turns away and I say quickly, "I could use your help."

He turns back with a glint on his eye.

"Name it."

"My sister."

Alessandro tenses and I feel a wicked thrill surge through me as I deal a hard blow in learning.

"Make her evening count but don't touch her. I'll owe you one."

Alessandro hisses beside me and I ignore him completely because fuck if I trust her with him, but Baron is different. He won't overstep the mark and will play his part because for some reason I trust him more than my own friends sometimes. We are two creatures born of the same soul. We understand one another and I know he won't let me down.

"Interesting. I heard your sister came to stay; did anything force that?"

"Just the usual kids' stuff but you could keep your eyes open and report anything you hear."

"Consider it done."

"Baron." A shout from the neighboring house claims his attention and he nods. "Duty calls. I'll see you later."

As he heads off, Alessandro snarls, "I don't trust him."

I say nothing because I do and that's all that counts.

13

WINTER

Emma is hyperventilating and rocking weirdly on the bed, her arms wrapped around her as if it's the only comfort she's got.

"I can't do this." Her eyes are wide and terrified, and I say gently, "It's fine. Just one drink and then we can slip away. Knowing my brother and his friends, they'll hook up with a girl and be otherwise occupied. Just stick with me. I won't let any harm come to you."

She swallows hard and groans. "I'll try."

"That's all I ask."

As she heads off to change, I feel so worried about my only friend. I'm used to this life. It's all I know, but all Emma has are the stories, legends and fear to feed off. She thinks these guys are monsters and rightly so. What she doesn't understand is the code of honor they live by. She wouldn't fear them half as much if she did because in our world, the only people we hurt are our enemies. Emma couldn't be anyone's enemy if she tried and so grudgingly, I admit Angelo is probably right to throw this party.

Knowing him, it was more for her benefit than mine because she needs to relax, or she'll end up in hospital or an institution.

Pulling on some jeans and a fresh top, I comb out my hair, letting it fall straight past my shoulders then make up my eyes in a smoky gray color and pull on my sneakers. Standard party issue wear, for me, anyway. No short skirts and definitely no cleavage. It always strikes me as hypocritical the way mafia men like their family members to dress conservatively, but their whores and mistresses to look like they charge by the hour. I'm pretty certain they'll be a lot of flesh on display tonight and yet I'm curious to attend my first proper college party, even if it is under the watchful eye of my brother and his annoying friends.

Then again, there's Alessandro. His wild beauty makes me burn and those dark hooded eyes are framed by the longest lashes I have ever seen on a man. I hope he wears his hair down tonight, instead of tied behind him because he looks a wild spirit, like the hero in a love story and I suppose that's why I'm making such an effort tonight—because of him.

I look for him when he's not in the room, wondering where he is, or who he's with. When he's there I feel him, every single breath, and if I had any choice in my life, it would be to end the evening in his arms. Just once. To understand what the big attraction is. To discover those special feelings when a man loves a woman and I want it to be with him. What do the guys constantly say? 'For one night only.' Maybe I could have that—with him.

Feeling more upbeat than earlier, I head off in search of Emma and smile when I see the effort she's made. Her jeans are smart and look new and she's tried to make up her face and cover the acne as best she can. A loose-fitting top hides her curves and her anxious eyes shine with a different light, telling me she's feeling a little of the excitement herself. Thinking about Flynn, I wonder if he can bring her out of her shell. Maybe that was Angelo's intention all along and I should give my brother some credit because even I know this atmosphere can't continue and maybe this party is just what we all need.

"Are you ready, honey?"

I smile at Emma, and she nods nervously. "I think so."

The music has been playing for the last hour and from the noise downstairs, I know we're not the first to arrive at our own party and as I head toward the staircase, she says breathlessly, "Please don't leave me, Winter."

"Not in a million years."

Grabbing her hand, I pull her after me and when we reach the top of the staircase, we pause and look through the rails, crouching low on our heels.

"Who can you see?" she whispers and I say quietly, "I see that girl I saved."

I peer a little closer. "She's quite pretty, despite the bruises."

"I heard she went with your brother." Emma whispers with a touch of reverence and I feel a surge of pity for the pretty girl who is looking around as if searching for someone.

Then I tense when I see the two girls from class and hiss, "I can't believe he invited those bitches."

"Who?"

"The girls who obviously hate me. You remember, the one with the jock who smashed the locker in your face and her friend who threatened me."

"Do you think they know we're here?"

Emma sounds as if she might cut and run, and a sudden feeling catches me that tells me their invitation was for a different reason entirely.

I almost pity them when I see my brother standing watching them and as the girls see him, I watch with interest as the girl heads his way, her hips swaying, no doubt sending him a very loud message.

"Watch." I nudge Emma and see the girl lean toward my brother, who is looking deadpanned as always and he says something and pushes her away, making her stumble a little before turning his back on her and chatting to a pretty girl by his side.

"Wow, that must have hurt."

Emma sounds in awe, and I sigh. "Typical behavior. Come on, we may as well get this over with."

Gripping Emma's hand hard, we head downstairs and straight to the kitchen, pushing past people who block the way until we find the coolers filled with beers.

"Want one?"

I place my hand on one to fling to my friend, but a large hand covers mine and I hear, "Not for you."

I look up and see Ivan frowning at me, and I sigh. "Are you really saying I can't drink at my own party?"

"No."

"Then let me go."

"You can drink water, bosses' orders."

"And Emma?"

"Same."

He reaches behind me and pushes some water into a glass from the tap on the fridge and holds it to my lips, trapping me in a wall of ink and menace.

"Drink, moy angel."

This feels so degrading and yet kind of sweet as I take a draft of the cool water he holds to my lips.

As he steps back, he nods to Emma, "Same."

He offers her the drink and then says in a deep drawl, "No alcohol; I'll be watching."

Grabbing Emma's arm, I pull her with me, saying angrily, "Fucking dictator. Who are you, my father?"

I catch a few nervous looks my way as other students witness the exchange, and I'm guessing they're not used to seeing anyone speak back to these guys. Ivan just shrugs and turns to a pretty girl by his side and hauls her against the wall, her legs wrapping around his waist, and proceeds to devour her in full view of the rest of us.

Emma starts shaking and, taking that as my cue to leave, I pull her with me from the room.

As we head inside the living room, I see a guy standing talking to Angelo who looks every bit as dangerous as my brother.

"Who's he?"

I nudge Emma and she shivers. "Baron Fitzgerald. He lives next door, but many think he should move in here."

"Why?"

"Because he fits in more. The other house is the one I told you about, where the rich kids go and have amazing parties. Maybe you should try for an invitation. I heard they're legendary around campus."

"Don't you want to go?"

"She shivers. "No. To be honest, I'm amazed I'm here at all. Just one hour though. I don't think I'll last past that."

Angelo looks up and beckons us over and with a sigh, I do what he says like the good little sister I am.

As we get closer to them, I feel the scrutiny of his friend, but unlike Alessandro, this guy just leaves me cold.

Angelo says evenly, "Come and meet Baron." He says to his friend, "This is my sister Winter and Emma, her friend." Baron looks interested. "Welcome to Rockwell. Angelo tells me we're now neighbors."

His voice has a strange accent that I can't place and yet he seems pleasant enough, so I smile.

"Yes, it appears that we are."

"You should come to our next party; both of you."

He looks between us, and Emma steps a little behind me as I say pleasantly, "Thanks, we might take you up on that."

"Only might?"

He looks amused, and Angelo laughs. "If she comes to one of your parties, I'm holding you responsible for looking after her, Baron."

"It would be my pleasure." His dark eyes flash with amusement and I feel myself relax. If Angelo likes him, then he can't be all bad, so I smile. "I'd like that."

Suddenly, the easy atmosphere is gone in a flash as I sense a scuffle behind me and then hear a loud scream and as I look into my brother's eyes, I watch his expression change in a heartbeat.

14

ANGELO

The music stops and everyone in the packed room turns to see what's happening and I feel my soul pant with expectation. This is what I love. What's molded into our souls and nurtured from a very young age. Pain, revenge, fear, and retribution. Qualities required to learn a trade many would die rather than experience for themselves.

Alessandro and Ivan have forced Eden and her friend Brianna into two chairs and are currently holding them in place by their hair and the fear in the girl's eyes is a magnificent sight to behold.

I don't enjoy hurting women; it doesn't sit right with me, but they need to be taught a lesson and it needs to be in full view of everyone to guarantee their humiliation.

Winter turns and looks at me and shakes her head.

She doesn't need to voice the words, it moves between us like a telepathic wave, and I feel my own eyes flash as I stare at her with a promise. 'This is for you.'

Slowly, I push off the wall and say in a low voice, "Have you anything to say?"

I address my question to Eden because we all know she is the ringleader in a gang that is terrorizing the female students for no other reason than to earn a reputation. She blinks the tears away as she looks at me helplessly and winces as Alessandro tightens his hold.

"I'm sorry." The tears burn in her eyes, and she looks deliciously helpless as she realizes her time's run out.

Her friend's tears are running down her face and she looks scared shitless, which suits my purpose and Ivan pulls down sharply on her hair and hisses, "Your turn."

"I'm sorry." She says it quickly and I almost laugh out loud because she doesn't even know what she's apologizing for. She just acts as a lookout most of the time and is nothing without her more dominant friend.

I address the room loudly. "Eden and Brianna made a fatal error when they targeted my sister and her friend. Brianna's guy paid the price, an eye for an eye, when he slammed a locker door into Emma's face."

The crowd gasps and all eyes turn to a quivering Emma who looks as if she's about to give up on life in seconds and I see Winter edge closer to offer reassurance. Flynn moves beside Emma and places his arm around her shoulder, and it amuses me to see the pure terror dawn in her eyes as she's caught between a rock and a hard place. This is a public claiming of the most fucked-up kind because the whole of Rockwell Academy knows Flynn doesn't care about anyone. However, tonight Emma is getting the full service and if she doesn't feel special by the time the dawn breaks, he won't have done his job.

I say roughly, "She is under our protection, so listen up.

Leave my sister and Emma alone or suffer the same fate as Eden and Brianna."

The terror dawning in their eyes wraps my soul in happiness because dealing with bullies is my favorite pastime. Girls like Emma don't deserve the way they are treated and need someone to stand up for them sometimes. I love pain and revenge, and we are taught to inflict it where it matters most. My sister is where it matters most, to me, anyway and so I say thoughtfully, "But what are we going to do to punish you?"

Brianna starts crying, and Eden looks shocked and completely mortified, which is amusing because we haven't even gotten started yet. I know most of what she does is to earn a reputation as a woman not to be messed with. She thinks that would impress me, would earn her passage as my girl and a place at my side. She knows shit because I don't do relationships of any kind and her night has passed and will never be repeated.

I turn to Winter. "It's your decision."

To her credit, she just looks bored, yet I know inside she will be hating this scene because Winter is a kind girl who hates violence. Ironic really when you think about where we come from.

"Any suggestions?" She throws it back at me and I laugh to myself. Getting her to seal another person's fate will be like discovering the tooth fairy, but I need everyone to see the power she holds. After tonight, nobody will mess with my sister and her time here will be drama free.

"I have a few. What about you Emma, what do you think their punishment should be?"

It's as if the devil has asked for her soul and Emma's frightened eyes blink in disbelief as Flynn's arm tightens around her shoulders and he strokes the back of her neck with a gentleness that always surprises me to witness.

Winter interrupts, "Emma won't want revenge. She's too good for that, but I'm different, not so kind and not as forgiving."

I knew she would step in to save her friend, which was my intention all along. To force Winter to face who she is and harden her heart. She needs to let go of sentiment to face the future, and it begins now.

"I want a promise from them both."

She glares at the girls and says with a voice edged in steel. "To stop intimidating the other students and trying to prove they're something they're not or will ever be."

"Too easy." I shake my head. "That will happen regardless. They need to pay the price for their actions and a promise just isn't good enough."

The atmosphere is tense, dark, and exciting. The other students are watching like vultures at an ancient battle. Horrified curiosity as they wait for the dramatic scenes that will prove how basic human behavior really is. A fight to the death before moving onto the next in line, a blood lust that can be more addictive than any drug.

Looking at Ivan, I say in a dead voice. "Ivan, do you have a preference?"

His eyes flash as he snarls, "I have several."

Brianna yelps as he twists her hair and forces her up to face him. "What will it take to teach you a lesson, I wonder? What will teach you not to fuck with my family?"

Alessandro grins and forces Eden's head down between her knees and growls, "I say we humiliate them and give them a visual reminder of their sins."

I can feel Winter's alarm from here and let it bathe my

tainted soul in pleasure. I love this. I feed off this, which shows me what a fucked-up animal I am.

I catch sight of Claudia's excited face staring at the scene with a flushed face and a bright gleam in her eye. She's loving this which is interesting. Maybe I misjudged her, and she's not as sweet as she looks.

Her eyes raise to mine, and I see an interest in them that would give me a night to remember and it's so tempting, so intoxicating, I almost consider breaking my own rule for one night only.

Laughing to myself, I look back at the two girls who await their fate with fear and resignation, and I snarl, "A temporary reminder will be sufficient payment. I think their vanity could use a lesson, cut off their hair."

The two girls' screams make me laugh as they face the worst possible outcome, in their eyes only.

Malik steps forward with a knife that would make an assassin's eyes water and as Alessandro holds Eden's hair in one hand, he slices through it, cutting it off close to the scalp. The shock ripples around the room as she cries as if she's been stabbed, and her screams of agony make me despise her even more.

Malik turns to Brianna who has the balls to plead with him, "Please, not my hair, not my face, I'm sorry, I'm ..."

Her tortured scream makes me smile as her own long, blonde hair joins Eden's on the ground and the gasps of horror all around me make me feel warm inside.

The sobs of the two girls are like music to my ears as Malik twists the metaphorical knife and says darkly, "Maybe we should shave the rest off."

The broken women moan with pain as if we have stabbed them in a frenzied attack, and I shrug. "What do you think, Winter? Do you think they've suffered enough, or do you want more? I mean, Claudia has a personal interest in this too. Maybe she wants more?"

All eyes turn to Claudia, who pales as the focus of the room shifts on her and she backs down, telling me she just isn't cut out for this. "No."

Her whisper irritates me a little and I say coolly, "Have it your way."

Heading over to Eden, I crouch before her shaking body and pull her chin to face me, relishing the beaten eyes that stare at me with humiliated defeat. "Just so everyone knows, you were a lousy fuck, and I regretted it the moment you spread your legs. Learn some self-respect and stop trying to make yourself feel good by terrorizing others. Oh, and by the way, you're no longer welcome here."

Nodding to Alessandro, he heaves her up and propels her across the room and as the crowd parts, they openly stare as she moves through them.

Alessandro opens the door and pushes her outside, slamming it behind her and then all eyes turn to Brianna who is sobbing, and I say bitterly, "You are even worse. You gain your reputation by another's actions. A look out and a cheerleader for the wrong team. Reveling in other people's pain, you are the worst kind of person. Never standing up for what's right and enjoying the misery of others. If anyone, I want to hurt you the most, but knowing how vain you are, this is the worst kind of punishment we could give you." Looking at Ivan, I snarl. "Throw the trash out."

He pulls her to her feet and almost drags her to the door before pushing her roughly outside and as the door slams, I snarl, "Show over." The music starts up again and I turn to my sister and see the sadness in her eyes that cuts me deeper than any knife could.

For a moment we are back at home, witnessing another punishment, another day at the office and I can tell she's wearied of it all. Then, like the good friend he is, Baron steps forward and rests his hand on her shoulder and whispers, "Hey, let me fetch you a drink."

She nods and turns with him, and I watch them head into the kitchen with the heaviest feeling in my heart. I'm not proud of what I did, but I will do worse if it means protecting her. She's all I've got, and I will never stop trying to make her life better in any way I can.

15

WINTER

I feel so empty. It's as if I'm numb inside and as Baron leads me to the kitchen, I follow him without really registering what's happening.

He hands me a cool glass of water and, unlike Ivan, smiles softly. "That was a hard scene to witness."

"It was." I sigh and lean against the counter. "They didn't deserve it."

"Are you sure about that?"

"Yes."

I shake my head. "They're just mean girls, that's all. Every school has them and probably always will. There are always bullies and Angelo just proved he's the biggest one around because that was wicked."

"Your brother was looking out for you."

"No, he just thinks he was."

I say sadly, "Angelo is the biggest bully of all. They all are because they get what they want by fear and intimidation rather than kindness. It's always been the same and I hate it."

"What would you have done in their position?"

"I don't know. Probably nothing. I'm guessing the right thing to do would be to report them and let the school deal with it through the right channels, but we both know that wouldn't solve the problem."

"Then you have your answer."

"Not really." I look at him with interest.

"What would you have done?"

He shrugs. "The same as Angelo, probably. You see, Winter, I don't have a sister; in fact, I don't have much of a family so I can't imagine what that feels like. But I do have friends who I would kill for. A kind of family of my own and so I understand a little. If one of them was threatened or upset in any way, I would do whatever it takes to remove the problem. As hard as it was, Angelo has taken away any power those girls thought they had. Their hair will grow again, but the memory will never fade and every student in the school will be laughing about this tomorrow."

"It's just ..."

"Cruel. Sometimes it's needed. Just think of how many other students your brother has saved from humiliation. Girls that don't deserve the attention of those bullies. He has ended the reign of one of them, and I'm guessing many would thank him for that."

"I guess." I say sighing. "I don't have to enjoy it, though."

Baron smiles and I kind of like the softer edge of my brother's friend and look at him with interest. "We have a lot in common, Baron."

"Maybe we do."

He pushes the cap off a beer and looks at me with curiosity. "Angelo tells me your life has been mapped out for you. How do you feel about that?"

"Like my life is over already."

The tears burn as I think about my future outside this house and Baron reaches across and lifts my face to his, and I'm surprised at the storm in his eyes.

"Listen to me, Winter, because I will only say this once. You are the boss of your own life, and you make the decisions in the end. Others may set you on one path, but how you walk it is up to you. Be smart, take it all in, learn how to survive and look for their weakness because there is always one. Then use that to your advantage to get what you want."

"I doubt that's an option for me, Baron. It would be like a mouse taking on a lion."

"The element of surprise is a powerful weapon, and I'm guessing you can learn to wield it where it will do the most damage. You are strong inside, and that counts for a lot."

I stare at him with a small spark of hope burning deep inside and he steps forward and whispers, "You are not alone. Your brother was right, family counts for everything and you have a powerful one. Then there's me."

"You?"

He nods, reaching up and stroking my face gently as he stares deep into my eyes. "You have me too. If it gets too much, come and find me. I don't live that far as it happens, and you may need a break from the madness on occasion. You're welcome to hang out with us anytime, no strings attached and just as friends."

His kindness undoes me in a way I'm not used to, and I hate the tears that show my weakness as they spill down my face. As he sweetly wipes them away, he says firmly, "Be strong, Winter and bide your time because you will have your day."

The door bangs open, and we turn to see Alessandro watching us with an angry look on his face and Baron laughs softly. "It appears that all the best parties end up in the kitchen, and I'm guessing this one is about to get even wilder."

As the room fills with students desperate to grab drinks, I stare at Alessandro with interest. The fact he looks heated, angry even makes me smile inside because now I see inside his soul. As he walks toward the cooler, his eyes don't leave me for a second and Baron whispers almost to himself, "Interesting."

I don't react because I can't tear my eyes away from the only man who has caught my attention this way. In a different life, I would be interested to see how far this could go with him, but we both know that isn't an option for me. I can look but never touch and that's part of the appeal, I suppose.

He reaches us and tears his eyes from mine and stares broodingly at Baron, who smirks. "You ok?"

Grabbing a can from the cooler, he opens it and chugs it down in one, before squeezing it tight and chucking it into the trash. "I'm always good."

Then he turns and walks away and Baron laughs. "He's got it bad."

"Got what? A drink problem?"

I laugh but we both know what he meant by that and I kind of like how that makes me feel. As if there's something here for me after all. That someone likes me outside of what I can do for them. Someone like Alessandro; someone I can never have.

Sighing, I smile at Baron. "Thanks. It was good to talk."

"Anytime."

He says with interest, "What happens now?"

"I rescue my friend."

He laughs out loud. "Good luck with that."

"What do you mean?"

"I doubt your friend will thank you for it."

"Then you don't know Emma."

I feel bad that I've left her even for a second, especially with Flynn hanging around with his wicked looks and dark intent.

"Come on." I roll my eyes. "I should save her, in any case."

The trouble is, when I head back into the room, Emma is nowhere to be seen.

16

ANGELO

Why do I feel like shit most of the time? Seeing Baron walk away with my sister doesn't make me feel any better. He gets to be the good guy —in her eyes, anyway, and I'm left to deal with the shit my life has dealt me.

"Angelo."

A soft voice makes me turn and I see Claudia looking at me with large, lust-filled eyes.

"Claudia."

I'm cool for a reason because she knows the score. I made it clear when she left the morning after we fucked all night. There would be no repeat performance.

She seems a little hesitant and then laughs nervously. "Thanks for that. I appreciated you sticking up for me."

"I did it for Winter."

"Yes, of course."

She looks nervous and I lean back against the wall.

"You got something to say?"

"I thought…"

"What, Claudia; what did you think?"

"That maybe we could..."

"I thought I made it clear the last time we met."

Her eyes fill with hurtful tears, and I sigh, feeling a little more generous than usual.

"Look, it was fun, but I'm not the dating kind of guy. I thought you knew."

"I'm not asking for a date." She shrugs. "Maybe just some company on the odd occasion with no strings."

"Sounds interesting, but no."

"Why not?"

"Because I don't form attachments and I don't want a regular girl because that wouldn't be fair on anyone. You see, as soon as college finishes, I'm out of here and you wouldn't like where I'm going. The best thing for everyone is to keep things casual and not catch feelings. It's best this way."

"It doesn't have to be like that. Everyone needs someone, even just a friend with, um, benefits."

I'm starting to get bored already and shake my head. "I'm not interested. Go and find that asshole of a boyfriend you had. I'm pretty sure he'll be a welcome distraction."

"We finished. *I* finished it." She sounds angry.

"Who wants to be with a guy like that when there are men like you in the world."

I almost laugh out loud. "Men like me, you don't know shit, Claudia. No woman in her right mind would want a man like me, no sane one, anyway."

I watch Flynn take Emma by the hand and lead her outside and Claudia says in surprise, "When were they a thing?"

"They're not. Flynn is looking out for Emma because she's family by default. Now, if you'll excuse me, I'm busy."

I turn my back on her and for the second time in less than an hour, I feel like the biggest bastard going.

Sometimes I think of taking a permanent girl. Someone to make me forget, someone to keep the bitches away. But it wouldn't be fair because I could never continue anything past college. It's best for everyone this way and so, as a pretty girl looks at me from across the room and smiles, I head over to her with only one thing on my mind.

"Hey." She smiles shyly and looks a little nervous, if I'm honest. I recognize her from history, not that Miss. English ever lets my attention wander from her, but I know who this girl is, and she's rumored to be dating Jefferson Michaels, one of the jocks. I'm curious why she's here, so I lean against the wall and fix her with an interested look. "Sammy, isn't it?"

She nods, her face flushing with pleasure, and I grin. "You sit across from me in history. I'm surprised to see you here."

"Are you?"

Fuck me, I'm bored already but she'll do to remove Claudia from my life, so I slam my hand beside her against the wall, imprisoning her in my personal space. "Have you got what you came here for?"

She licks her lips nervously, "Not yet."

"And Jefferson, what does he think about his girl partying on the bad side of town?"

For a moment, her eyes cloud with bitterness and her smile slips. "He's probably banging a cheerleader in the bleachers. He wouldn't care."

"So, you thought you'd get even."

"Maybe."

She looks nervous now and I grin. "A fuck for a fuck, maybe."

"Maybe."

"One night only, no coming back."

"Really?" She licks her lips. "Maybe I like the sound of that."

Lifting my hand, I run my thumb across her lips and hear the door bang and instinctively know a rather disgruntled former lay is storming from the building.

Leaning in, I capture her lips with mine and deal a punishing kiss that can't be pleasant. I bite her lip to draw blood and fist her hair to cause pain. I push in hard and kick her legs apart and run my hand up her tight top, cupping her tit in my hand and twisting her nipple. I don't care we are putting on a show and that video footage of Jefferson's girl is probably heading his way right now. All that concerns me is proving a point. I don't need anyone, I can have anyone, I have no heart.

Her moans of desire tell me she's enjoying every minute of this and so I whisper, "Do you want me to fuck you against this wall or go somewhere more private."

Her eyes widen in surprise as she says quickly, "Private."

"I thought so."

Grabbing her hand, I push her through the open door behind us, but not to the staircase. This is going to be quick. Instead, I push her outside and pull her behind a bush.

"What here?" She doesn't look too pleased about that, and I whisper, "Live dangerously, Sammy. Don't settle for normal, experience abandonment."

I suck her neck until she moans, and I run my hand

under her short skirt and feel a bare drenched pussy begging to be filled.

Hoisting her leg over my arm, I push her against the weather-boarded side of the house and unzip my pants with the other hand. Fishing for a condom, I make short work of it and as I push inside, I place my hand across her mouth to stifle her grunt of desire. Thrusting, deep and hard, I relish the feeling it gives me. A willing woman and no strings attached, just how I like it. I make sure to leave my mark across her neck and her scream of release can be heard across the darkened space, carried off by the wind, telling me she loved every minute of it.

Unlike Claudia, this is a revenge fuck and doesn't require a softer approach. She's got what she came here for and helped me solve another problem. Girls like Sammy don't think things through and if she thought a night in my bed was on the cards, she's going to be disappointed. I have used her like a cheap whore because she came begging for it and doesn't deserve anything else. Maybe she'll learn a lesson from this, maybe not, but it killed a few minutes of my time and sharpened my reputation as a bastard. Job done.

Pulling back, I zip up my pants and take a moment to admire the sight of a woman who has just come all over my cock. Her eyes are bright, her skin flushed and her breathing hard and labored.

We hear giggling as a group of girls pass by and I'm guessing they witnessed the whole sordid act and I wonder how Sammy will deal with the looks she gets in the morning as everyone learns what a whore she really is.

"Thanks for the fuck. See you around."

I move away and she says in disbelief, "What? That's it."

"You expecting anything else?"

"But..." Her voice breaks and I couldn't give a fuck because if she thought this was true love, she's deluded.

Heading back around the house, I take the front steps and see Flynn and Emma sitting on the swinging seat. His arm is draped across her shoulders and his head bent to her ear and her laughter rings out as he whispers his usual shit.

They look up as I stop and say to her, "You ok, Emma?"

She just nods, looking at me as if Satan has come calling, and I nod to Flynn. "Catch you later."

His smirk tells me everything I need to know and for a moment, I feel a surge of love for my psychotic friend. This is just as good for him, almost as much as it will be for her, and I hope they can share demons and conquer them together.

17

WINTER

I'm feeling anxious because I can't see Emma anywhere. She's not in the kitchen or the living room and even when I went to our rooms and looked for her, it was obvious she hadn't been there either.

When I head downstairs, I find Alessandro watching me with a brooding expression and an air of boredom. I notice another can in his hand and the slight redness to his eye and wonder how many he's had. A girl is trying to engage his attention, but he is staring at me as if the demons are circling and, rather than feel anxious, it just wraps me in safety, familiarity, and home.

He completely ignores the girl and pushes past, and her face falls when she sees me approaching.

"Have you seen Emma?"

I don't know why I think he'd tell me anything, and I was right, because he shrugs. "No."

Sighing heavily, I make to push past him, and he blocks my escape, leaning down and growling ominously, "Where are you going?"

"To find Emma, of course. Surely that's obvious."

"Where's, Baron?"

He doesn't seem to want to know about anything else, and I shrug. "I don't know. I'm looking for my friend. Maybe he's doing the same."

He leans in, whispering darkly, "Leave her, she's fine."

"How do you know, unless..."

I feel the realization hit me because for fuck's sake, they promised.

"Where's Flynn?"

He smirks. "Maybe he's found a friend to play with."

"Emma?" My heart fills with anger and he grins, backing me against the wall and crowding my space. "Leave her. She's safe and won't thank you for it."

"What have you done? Where is she?"

I try to look around him, but his body is one mass of solid muscle, and he must be well over six feet tall. The fact his hair hangs wild, and his eyes are feral, makes my heart beat faster as he whispers huskily, "I'm your bodyguard, sweetheart, and there is nowhere left to run."

"Why would I run?"

"To help your friend, to save the world, how the fuck do I know what you think, but I've been assigned your personal guardian angel along with the rest of them and I take my duties extremely seriously."

He is so close, I can feel the heat from his body as it mixes with aftershave and cigarettes along with the scent of alcohol on his breath.

"You're drunk."

I state the obvious and he grins, his eyes flashing, which is a serious turn on that I could really do without right now.

"Guilty as charged."

For some twisted reason, I'm enjoying being the focus of his attention and I know as soon as Angelo sees us, he'll tear us apart, so I say innocently, "Why don't I get you some fresh air?"

"Is that what you want, sweetheart, fresh air?" He laughs out loud, and I nod. "Yes, I think you could use some."

Smiling, I push him gently away and guide him through the back door and hear sobbing coming from around the back of the house.

Alessandro sobers up almost instantaneously and grabs my arm, pulling me behind him. We turn the corner and I see a girl crouched on the ground against the side of the house, tears streaking her face.

"Are you ok?" I feel concerned and wonder what happened, and she shakes her head. "Not really."

Alessandro growls and I fix him with a withering look. "Back off."

Dropping to my knees, I say kindly, "Would you like to clean up inside? I could fetch someone if you like."

It's obvious she's been fooling around, and I hope to God it wasn't against her will and she sobs. "No one can help me."

I look at Alessandro in surprise and he shrugs and turns away. Bastard.

"I can help you." I try to remain calm, but inwardly I'm so angry on her behalf. Whoever did this left her discarded in the dirt and that will never be ok with me.

"I just want to go home."

"I'll walk with you then."

Alessandro's irritated sigh causes me to snap, "We can't leave her."

"Fine, then let's get this over with."

I help her to her feet, and she looks at me with a lot of embarrassment as she brushes the dirt from her legs and tries to wipe the tears from her face.

"You must think I'm an idiot."

"I don't think anything."

We start walking toward the cheerleader's house, and I wonder why she came at all. She doesn't seem the type to enjoy one of Angelo's parties and as Alessandro follows like the Grim Reaper behind us, silent and deadly, I whisper, "Do you want to talk about it?"

She glances nervously behind her. "No, it's fine. I'm just feeling like a bit of a fool, really."

"Don't beat yourself up about it; we all do things we regret in the morning."

Wishing I had that luxury, I sigh heavily. "You'll be fine."

She nods and says with a slight break to her voice, "I wish your brother was as kind as you."

My heart drops. Angelo.

"Did he do this to you?"

I feel sick inside as she nods and leans closer so Alessandro can't hear her. "It was my idea and I kind of pushed him into it, but he was so cold, brutal even and then walked away, leaving me there."

"Why did you let him?" I'm more curious than judgmental, and she sighs. "I had an argument with my boyfriend because I heard he fucked one of my friends under the bleachers. I wanted to hit him where it hurt, I suppose."

"That's disgusting, him I mean."

"Yes, it is, but I was no better. I went to that party

hoping for what I got and the fact it happened is down to me. The trouble is, it's not that much of a secret and I'm guessing the entire school will be disgusted with me in the morning and he will drop me anyway, probably hooking up with Susan instead."

"Is that your friend?"

We stop outside the house, and she sighs heavily. "She was." Turning to face me, her eyes are bright as she whispers, "You know, it sucks when you lose your best friend and your guy in one moment of madness. Anyway, thank you. You helped when you didn't need to, and I appreciate that."

"Yes, it did. Losing your friend more than your guy, I mean." I smile. "What will you do now?"

She looks at the house and shakes her head. "Clean up my act, ditch my boyfriend, and concentrate on graduating. What else can I do? I'm my own worst enemy, Winter. I shouldn't be let out at night."

The door opens, and a girl looks out into the darkness and whispers loudly, "Sammy?"

"Is that Susan?" I ask because the pain on Sammy's face tells me she's dealing with shit right now and she nods. "Yes."

The girl runs down the steps and looks at us hesitantly, glancing nervously behind us at Alessandro, who is a large forbidding shadow of menace.

She looks as if she's been crying and her voice shakes as she whispers, "I'm sorry, please forgive me."

Sammy just steps forward and pulls her in for a hug and I hear her say softly, "Come on, we need to talk."

As they turn to head inside, I feel a pang of longing for a close friend like that. Someone who obviously cares and is there when I need them. Whatever happened with Sammy's boyfriend is obviously not as important as their friendship and I'm glad about that and as they head up the steps, Sammy turns and says gratefully, "Thanks, Winter. You're welcome here anytime. Just don't bring your brother."

Her laughter reassures me and as the door closes, Alessandro steps beside me and says gruffly, "I'll never understand women."

"In what way?"

"If my best friend screwed my girl, I'd knock him dead. Not comfort him when he apologizes."

I smile to myself. "I think they've got it right. Unlike the rest of you who use women with no regard for their feelings."

"Feelings." Alessandro laughs bitterly. "Feelings are for people who have that luxury. We don't."

Turning, he grabs my arm and growls, "We should be getting back. The last thing I need is your brother thinking I'm doing the same with his sister."

"You leave my brother to me."

I feel so sick when I think of Angelo using Sammy like a cheap whore, and yet I'm not surprised. My father is his only example in life, and he would have done far worse.

"Don't you wish it was different, Alessandro?"

I'm curious because I'm guessing his life is much like ours, and he growls. "Every fucking minute of my life."

I'm curious about what that involves and can't resist saying, "What will you do when you leave college?"

"Same as Angelo, probably."

He doesn't seem inclined to talk and I wonder if

anything gets through to these guys, but I keep on trying, anyway. "Will you return to Italy?"

He laughs bitterly. "My family live in Boston now. Only my grandfather remains in Italy. My father decided he preferred new territory and set up there. I'm expected to fall into line and be the good son, but my grandfather wants me back in Italy to replace him when he's gone."

"How do you feel about that?"

"Like I'd rather cut off my own balls and live like a monk rather than bury myself in the homeland and deal with what that involves."

"Can you refuse?"

He stops and his dark eyes flashing is the only emotion I see as he hisses, "I never had you down for a fool, Winter."

"I'm not." I feel my anger rising and he leans in so close I almost take a step back as he invades my personal space, causing a shiver of desire to run through my body because Alessandro is everything I dreamed of, standing right before me looking as if he wants to devour me on the spot.

"I want my freedom. To live life under my own terms and conditions and have the freedom of choice. I don't want to live in fear of never seeing the sunrise and wondering if this is my last day on earth. I want to be allowed to choose my own wife and my own career and not live under the shadow of pain and I don't want to join the family business where drugs, sex and arms deals are spoken about on a fucking agenda every morning."

He looks so lost and I know how that feels, so I reach out and touch his broad shoulder and whisper, "What would you choose if that freedom was yours?"

For a second, his eyes burn with a longing that makes

me shiver inside, and he leans closer and says, almost as if he's somewhere else, "I want to make movies. Lose myself in a world where I can make anything happen. Take life and mold it to my dreams and live out fantasy. I want to drive away reality and I want to run as far away from my birth right as possible. But right now, Winter, in this moment, standing in the darkness, I want to the freedom to love you."

I step back in surprise and his words hit me hard. *He feels it too.*

This upsets me more than anything because now he's voiced something I only imagined; it makes it harder to resist. Edging a little closer, I daren't look into his eyes and whisper, "Maybe we can have that, Alessandro, for one night only."

His deep breathing makes me look up and what I see drives a stake through my heart. The longing, the pain, and the emptiness mirrors my own and tentatively he reaches up and allows my dark hair to filter through his fingers and just feeling his touch makes me stand as if frozen to the spot.

I shiver inside as he pulls me toward him carefully and leans closer, his lips hovering dangerously close to mine and it would be so easy to step a little closer and into his heat, feeling him close around me like a safety net. His lips brush against mine and I feel the desire drench my reasoning as we hover between ruin and salvation and he whispers, "One kiss would start a war that I wouldn't survive."

"I know."

The pain in my heart is hard to deal with because we can't even enjoy the freedom college was meant to bring us.

But I can't let go and whisper with desperation, "Just one kiss to remind me I'm human, that's all I ask."

I know he's struggling, but I want this so badly I don't stop to think about that and my heart falls when he pulls away abruptly. "One kiss changes history, Winter and if I thought it would change ours, I'd go there like a Rocketship, but it will just complicate an increasingly complicated situation."

"Why is it complicated?"

I can't let this moment go and he says angrily, "Because I want you and you know it. I want to protect you, to love you and to be given a chance of happiness with you but I'm a fool if I think that's an option, so once again, I'm falling in line and being the good soldier because I will not start something I can't finish."

"A kiss. You won't even give me that."

I know I sound like a weak, petulant child and completely understand how Sammy got herself into the mess earlier. It appears common sense is abandoned when desire takes over and I'm surprised when he lifts my face to his and says gently, "I want to kiss you so badly I can hardly breathe. I've never met anyone like you, Winter. Beautiful, strong and brave. Kind and considerate despite the horrors you've witnessed, and it makes me feel almost human seeing you deal with your shit life when I need the bottle to make me forget mine. I want what you have, Winter, in every way, and I have a feeling that one kiss is all it would take to ruin me forever."

"I've never been kissed, Alessandro, never had that luxury. Maybe I will never know what it feels like to kiss a man I want more than air. Maybe it was never going to be my pleasure to enjoy, and I shouldn't ask for something that will ruin me too. But I need to know what that feels like to remind me I'm human when…"

I break away because the thought of my first kiss with a monster is too frightening to think about and so I'm surprised when a strong hand wraps around my head and pulls me toward him and as his lips claim mine, hell freezes over for the briefest second and stops burning.

His kiss is soft, possessive, and dominant, yet the sweetest taste in the world. His lips are soft against mine and I love how his tongue claims mine, licking, sucking, and tasting as if he can't get enough. I feel his hard body pressed against me as he pulls me close and just feeling him harden makes me long for more. We share a never-ending kiss, at least I wish it was and as we kiss under the stars, I can almost believe in magic. Soft, then hard, slow, then fast, we make this kiss count, knowing it's our first and last. Out here in the shadows, we can be anyone we want to be and as we enjoy that feeling for once in our lives, forbidden desires are indulged that should never had been allowed to blossom into something that will go no further. Yes, for one night only, Winter Sontauro is a normal girl, kissing a man who she wants more than anything in life and for the briefest moment, it feels like heaven.

18

ANGELO

The anger builds the longer I sit on the porch and wait for my sister. Flynn and Emma have left, and the party is carrying on inside. I feel pissed and want them to leave, but Ivan and Malik are intent on making the most of it and I know they need to cut loose for one night. The clock is ticking and even though we have a tentative plan in place for our future, it won't change the profession.

Mafia. How I hate that word. That life and that birthright.

I watch them head toward the house and feel so angry I can taste nothing but revenge and as they step into the light, I look eagerly for any sign telling me I need to vent my rage on my close friend.

Instead, they walk slightly apart and if anything, Winter looks angry, in a rage even, and I wonder what happened between them.

As they head up the steps, I snarl, "Where the fuck have you been?"

Winter says in an angry voice, "Fuck you, Angelo, you don't get to play the big brother card, not after what you've done."

"What I've done. Are you kidding me? You're the ones sneaking around in the darkness, and I wonder why?"

I stand and move toward them and am surprised when Alessandro throws me a warning look, telling me I'm about to be handed my balls by my own sister as she faces me, her eyes blazing.

"I thought you were better than that, Angelo?"

"You have to be more detailed, Winter, because I haven't got a fucking clue what you're talking about."

"Sammy."

I nod as all becomes clear and I shrug. "What about her?"

"You used her and left her sobbing in the dirt. You acted just like our father, and I am so disappointed in you."

Her words almost amuse me, and I look at Alessandro and say roughly, "Leave us."

He throws me a pitying look as he nods and heads silently into the house and I snarl, "Not here. Come inside. We need to talk about this in private."

She follows me around the back of the house, and we slip inside, using the back staircase to reach the second floor and I open the door to the gym and usher her inside.

Jerking my head toward the boxing ring Ivan and Alessandro love to spar in, I say almost with amusement, "Shall we fight it out?"

"If I thought I'd win, I'd take you up on that."

Sinking to the floor, I pull her down with me and just like back home, we sit side by side with our backs against the wall and she rests her head on my shoulder.

"Why did you treat her like that, Angelo? I thought you were better than our father."

"What makes you think that?"

"Because I know you hate him, what he does and how he goes about it. Why fuck a girl and leave her crying in the dirt? It's something he would do?"

Closing my eyes, I lean back against the wall and say bitterly, "I'm nothing like him. Sammy came to me for a revenge fuck. She didn't want me, just the weapon to throw back in her boyfriend's face. No strings attached and for one night only. I was up front about that, and she could have walked away with no regrets. She knew the score and the fact she couldn't deal with how that made her feel afterward is probably the reason why you found her sobbing with regret."

"You could have..."

"Could have what, Winter?" I sigh heavily. "Told her I loved her, that I would care for her, love her and make the bad things in life go away. Make her my girl and parade her around campus like loves young dream. We both know that is never going to happen and certainly not after a quick fuck against the wall at a fucking college party. Girls like Sammy know exactly what they're doing when they come inside minus their underwear, looking for something they can't live with in the morning. We meet girls like that every day and that won't change in the outside world. This is my life, Winter and yours is even worse."

I remind her of the harsh reality of our fate, and she says in such a sad voice I want to smash something. "It's so hard seeing what we could have if we were allowed to choose."

My heart tightens with an unbearable pain as I imagine

her future. Married to a fucking monster who will treat her worse than I did Sammy. Use her to bear the next generation of mafia slaves and sentence her to a life in a gilded cage. No freedom, just abuse, and we both know there is nothing we can do about that all the time our father is alive.

"What happened with Alessandro? Do I need to kill him?"

She laughs, which brings a brief smile to my lips. "I like him and if things were different…"

"But they're not."

I harden my voice because sentiment will just make her weak, and she sighs. "If I could choose a different life, I would head somewhere where I could be free. Maybe work as a nurse, help others and live in a little weather-boarded house by the sea with a man who chops logs for a living, not people."

"With a family of four children and three dogs and two cats."

I remind her of the perfect life she imagined in our childhood, and she laughs. 'He has a boat and brings fish home for a cookout. We have a wide circle of friends and enjoy vacations in Europe."

"I visit with my own wife and two kids who are just like me."

"And I'm the best aunt there is, spoiling them with chocolate and corn dogs and tales of how annoying their father was as a child."

We laugh, and I'm happy that just for a moment, the tense cloud lifts, and we can imagine a normal life outside of the one looming ever closer.

She sighs and says in the voice of an angel. "That's why I hated what you did earlier. This time is special, and we can be anyone we want to be away from the madness. I want you to experience love for once in your life, Angelo, something to remember when you step into the family business."

"I have love in my life and that's what's killing me inside."

Once again, the darkness circles me like the hungriest vulture, as I say with a voice devoid of emotion. "Love weakens a man and gives his enemies a way to destroy him. They take what you care about the most and use it against you. It's why we're taught not to feel. To shut away our heart to survive. I have a weakness and it's you and everyone knows that. That's what keeps me up at night. Makes me shut down any emotion. The thought of anyone hurting you because of me is like a permanent knife twisting in my heart. I can't add another knife to that. I would be dead within a week. I need to be cold for my own survival, and I thought you knew that."

She takes my hand and laces her fingers with mine and for a while we just sit as we have done a million times before. Two hearts created from the same embryo. As close as two people can get courtesy of our DNA and weaker because of it. I want the best for my sister, I always have and the best thing for her is to keep her safe. Deliver her to her future as agreed and work out a way to bring her back to me before the damage is done. And I don't have long because Winter's day of reckoning will happen the minute she graduates and I expect the man collecting her from the gates won't be our father.

19

WINTER

The next day, I almost run to Emma's room because she wasn't there when I hauled my ass to bed last night. Just the bump in the bed tells me she's sleeping way past her usual alarm of 6 am.

"Emma." I whisper as if I'm afraid of what state she'll be in and all I get in return is a soft groan. "It can't be morning already. Go to bed."

Jumping on the bed, I shake her awake. "It's 9 am already. We'll be late for class."

"What the..." The comforter falls back as she sits up in a panic and rubs her eyes in astonishment. "Oh my god, why didn't my alarm wake me, why didn't you wake me and why didn't God wake me?"

She makes to jump out of bed, and I pull her back, laughing. "It's fine. It won't matter if you're late. It's a study period anyway and we can make it up at lunch."

"It's still not right."

She groans and falls back against the headboard and as I stare, she raises her eyes. "What?"

"You."

"What about me?"

I shake my head. "I don't know, you look different somehow and I can't put my finger on…"

I slap my hand to my mouth, and she says with a puzzled frown, "What?"

"You didn't…"

"Didn't what?"

'Flynn."

"What about him?"

"Did he?"

"What?"

Groaning, I shake my head. "I'll ask you a direct question and you had better answer it. Did you have sex with Flynn last night?"

"No. Oh my god is that what everyone thinks?"

She looks so worried it makes me laugh. "Relax, nobody's said a thing. It's just I saw the way he looked at you and, well, I suppose I feared the worst."

Emma has a small smile on her lips, and she sighs, her eyes glazing over as she says dreamily. "I really like Flynn, Winter. He was so kind, protective even, and I never knew he was so funny."

Just thinking of my brother's slightly deranged friend, I wonder if we're talking about someone else entirely.

Settling back under the covers, she laughs softly. "You know, he made me feel so special, beautiful even. He paid me so many compliments and made sure I was warm enough, brought me drinks and made sure nobody even got close. He's such an angel."

"So I've heard." I shake my head because what the hell

is going on here? He doesn't seem the type at all, and I wonder what he's playing at.

"So you didn't..."

"No, but you know what, I kind of wished we had."

I just stare at her in total shock. "You *are* my friend Emma, aren't you? You know, the scared one who had to be dragged here under protest?"

She giggles and I don't think I've ever seen her look so pretty. Wow, Flynn must have the magic touch because she's a completely different person from yesterday.

Shrugging, I make to leave, and she pulls me back and whispers, "He asked if I'd ever been with a man before; just brought it up in conversation, along with the weather."

"What did you say?"

I settle back down, and she grins. "No, of course. I mean, nobody even looks at me, let alone wants to, well, you know."

She smiles as if she has a delicious secret to keep safe.

"He told me if I ever wanted to know what it felt like to ask him. One night only because he doesn't want to form attachments. He said he would show me how amazing sex could be with the right person and couldn't bear to think of me having a shit first time."

"He really said that?" My mouth drops open and she sighs. "He did and you know something even more surprising ..."

"What?" I hold my breath as she whispers, "I'm considering it."

"With Flynn."

I can't believe what I'm hearing, and she giggles. "Why not. He's made it pretty clear there would be nothing in it.

Just a lesson in love to educate me and you know how much I value education, Winter."

Once again, she giggles, which makes me smile. "You know, honey, if that's what you want, I think you should go for it. Just remember what he said and don't expect anything past that one experience. You know how they are. Their fucking motto is 'one night only' and I think they say it aloud, so it convinces them more than anyone."

She nods. "The only thing holding me back is how I'd feel the next day. Would I regret it, feel like a fool? Maybe he's using me and is just setting me up for a hard fall. It wouldn't surprise me because guys are always messing with me and treating me as if I don't matter."

Resting my hand on her arm, I smile. "I don't think Flynn's like the rest of them, not by a long way. I just don't want to see you get hurt, that's all."

"Do you think it hurts? I kind of think it must."

"Who knows for sure, but we'll find out one day. At least you can control your first time. Some of us don't even own that part of them."

She looks sad. "You don't talk about your home life much. Mind you, neither do I. Is there any way you can leave, maybe head somewhere else and start fresh?"

"Nice thought, but no. You see, Emma, you're right to fear my brother and his friends. We all share a hard upbringing in common and our fathers want us in the family business straight after graduation."

"What business?"

"Best you don't ask."

She looks afraid. "But surely…"

"No, Emma. I know what you're going to say, and we don't have a choice. Angelo will join the family business and I will marry into a rival one. It's how life works for us and there is nothing we can do about that."

I sigh heavily. "You think living here is bad, that the guys are bad and you're probably right, but honey, this is nothing because outside these walls, real life is one hundred times worse. So, enjoy Flynn's attention and make it count because that guy is right to keep you at a distance, for his own sake and yours too, because if you get caught up in this life, yours may not last long."

She says nothing and despite the fact we never talk about our families, I kind of think she knows exactly what I mean and then she says with a hint of defiance in her voice, "Then I'll study law and make it big in Boston. I'll help you all; you can count on me."

"Thanks, honey." I smile as if I really believe she can make a difference. "You do that."

As I head off to change, I feel happy that she's here. At least I know what it's like to have a friend. She'll never believe me, but I can count on one hand how many actual friends I have, and she is the best one yet. Most of them like me for my connections. In my last school I was isolated mainly, but I had a group of friends I drifted along with. Girls who never fit in who allowed me to join their club because I couldn't bear to mix with the popular girls and learn how easy their own lives were. I feel most at home with girls like Emma who never seem to catch a break because I'm one of them. At least I think so.

LUCKILY, the guys are sleeping in, and we manage to get out of the house without any unwanted questions, and yet I saw the disappointment in Emma's eyes when she found Flynn missing. I wonder how long before she claims her one night with him. I'm guessing not long because, like me, she's probably curious what it involves. My opinion of him changes the more I get to know him, and I genuinely believe he wants to make her feel special. He's an angel of course and even fallen ones like him hide a good heart behind the madness and part of me hopes he lives up to the reputation. For her sake, anyway.

20

WINTER

Our study period is over, and I head to history, bumping into Sammy on the way. She's walking with the friend I saw her with last night and she calls me over. "Hey, Winter!"

I head their way thinking how strange this all is, to me, anyway, and when I reach them, Sammy says in a whisper, "Word is out about Eden and Brianna. Apparently, they're not in class and the video has gone viral. I wouldn't want to be them right now."

Susan nods. "I can't believe that happened. In fact, I can't believe anything that happened last night, especially you, Sammy."

I look at her sharply because I wonder what she told her friend, and she shrugs, looking slightly guilty. "It was a moment of madness, but the kind of madness that makes you want a repeat performance."

Susan shakes her head. "I wonder what Jefferson will say. He's bound to have heard by now."

"He has."

Sammy's smug grin is at odds with how I left her last night and it strikes me she's enjoying the notoriety a little too much for my liking.

"He called this morning and wants to talk. He's as mad as a jealous dog and wants to sort things out."

Looking at her friend, I notice the pain in her eyes and wonder about their friendship. Three's a crowd and certainly when it concerns a guy and I wonder what will happen between them. Both girls have given themselves up for a casual fuck against a wall and any sympathy I had for Sammy is decreasing by the second.

"I should, um, go." I try to get away, but Sammy says cheerily, "Max is throwing a party tomorrow night. Why don't you come, bring that guy of yours too?"

"He's not my guy."

Just the thought of it makes me sad because of how amazing that would be.

"Then bring a friend, but please say you'll come. They throw the best parties and I'm sure you'll find someone to hook up with. Most of the team go there and Max's friends are seriously hot, not to mention the man himself. Now there's a cock I would love to ride."

She laughs and I say awkwardly, "Anyway, um, thanks. Yes, I'll see you there."

I quickly turn away because this conversation is making me uncomfortable and any pity I had is fading fast because it appears my brother was right. Sammy did plan that all along, and he was the best weapon of revenge she could wield.

I HEAD to history and take my seat, trying not to make eye contact with anyone. It's hard being the sister of the college bully and people either hate me or want to be my friend to get close to him.

Miss. English heads inside with a bright smile, looking like a cute mom off Netflix.

I wonder if she knows how lucky she is. She's probably got it all worked out. A sweet loving boyfriend with a good job and a house full of lovely things, with exotic vacations when semester ends.

By the end of the lesson, I feel as if I have the world on my shoulders and as I stand wearily, she says loudly, "May I have a word, Winter?"

"Sure." I'm surprised because I don't think I've missed any assignments and as the last student leaves, she closes the door and says pleasantly, "Is everything ok, honey?"

"Why wouldn't it be?"

She perches on the edge of her desk and looks like the big sister I never had as she smiles sweetly. "It's just I can sense that you're unhappy and wondered if I can help. I'm sure you've got friends and people to turn to, but I understand you're living with your brother and his friends. That can't be easy."

"It's fine." I'm guarded around strangers, especially when it concerns my brother, and even though she's probably just being kind, I give nothing away.

Her smile is like a breath of fresh air because I react well to kindness, never having experienced much of it in my life so far and she says in a gentle voice, "I want you to know that I'm here for you. Someone you can talk to, off the record. An older woman who won't judge, just listen and if there's anything worrying you, or hard to deal with, know I'm on your side."

"Thank you."

I look down because it would be so good to offload this problem onto someone else. A person of authority who may just be able to help. In wild moments of foolishness, I almost believe that's all it would take. A word in the right ear, someone to take me under their wing and call the authorities in to remove me from my father's care. Then I wake up and realize there's nobody on earth powerful enough to make that happen because the moment I leave, he would hunt me down and bring me right back home. The best way to deal with my father and my situation is to bide my time. Keep my head down and hope to God Angelo has a plan because the future's looking dark for me and I doubt Miss. English could ever imagine what that feels like.

She says kindly, "You should head to your next class, but take this." She hands me a small, printed card. "It's my details and if you ever need me, just call."

"Why me, Miss. English?" I'm puzzled about that, and she says softly, "Because I see the unhappiness in your eyes and I can't bear it. Like you, I had a difficult upbringing. My father was cold and aggressive and beat my mom."

I'm surprised to hear that, and it must show because she shrugs. "Don't let your childhood define you as a person. It's such a fleeting moment in a person's life. As soon as I could, I ran away and headed to the furthest point I could and worked my way through college and into teacher training. I took charge of my life and have never regretted a second of that." She sighs. "I suppose I see myself in you. The girl I was when I thought the world was against me. It doesn't have to be that way and from one runaway to possibly another, I can tell you now, the world isn't half as scary as they have you believe. There's so much we can do to disappear, and I know all the tricks, so, what do you say, come to me if you need my help, or just to vent. Either way, I'm here for you."

She stands and reverts to the teacher she is as her next class files through the door.

"You may go, Winter. Think on what I've told you."

I head out past the curious stares and whispered words and blink away the tears before they reveal my weakness to the rest of them. Could it be that easy? Part of me wants to try at least. Maybe not all hope is lost, after all.

"You took your time."

Looking up, I'm surprised to see Malik waiting for me, looking antsy and the dark shadow in his eyes makes me shiver. He terrifies me because of all of them, he's the unknown. A dark, disturbing force to be reckoned with, an assassin and a deadly weapon. Maybe it's his Arabic features and hooded eyes. Maybe it's the piercing gaze that makes you feel he knows your secrets way better than you. A master manipulator and destroyer of souls; it certainly feels like that.

"Why are you here?" I feign boredom as he falls into step beside me.

"You've got a problem."

"Tell me something I don't know."

I'm mildly curious though and sigh. "Ok, what is it?"

"Angelo."

"What about him?"

He wants you back at the house. Someone slipped a note under the door last night and it's not looking good for you."

My heart starts thumping and I feel the panic rising. "What note? What does it say?"

"Ask your brother. I'm just the one making sure you get there."

As we walk, I try to distract my mind from whatever this could be and side eye my escort.

"What's your plan after graduation?"

"Head home, take my place in the family business. Usual shit."

"Where's home?"

"Dubai."

"Wow, that's far. Why did they send you here?"

"To make connections."

"And have you?"

"Yes, but maybe not the ones they hoped for."

He laughs softly and almost appears human for a second.

"Do you mind going back?"

"Not really. It's my home and familiar. Then again, I couldn't give a shit if I never saw it again either. You see, I've never set down roots and have an urge to travel, anyway."

"Then why don't you?" I'm curious to see if Malik is as much a prisoner as the rest of us, and he shrugs. "I might."

"And if you go home, what will that involve?"

He stops and as he turns, I see the same madness in him that they all share.

"Violence, pain and imprisonment." He laughs bitterly. "Trapped in a loveless marriage and drawn into darker dealings that make your own look like fairy stories. Murder, intimidation and plans to bring down kings and continents. Wealth is all that matters in my country and making sure you have more than anyone. That is my future; sound familiar, Winter."

My heart sinks because we are all the same. At least I don't live with the horror that their jobs will bring. I just need to deal with the sexual and mental abuse, so I suppose I've got off lightly, which makes me smile.

"Do you find that funny, Winter?"

"Sorry." I shake my head. "I was just thinking I get off lightly compared to your future and the rest of them. It made me laugh to think my future was better than yours."

He nods. "We're all dreading graduation day. None of us really have control of our lives. We do as we're told because there is no other option. The trick will be to do it better than anyone else, and then maybe we have a chance to change things."

He appears a little warmer somehow and whispers, "I have two words to prepare you for what's coming."

"What are they?" My heart starts thumping and he whispers, "The Kiss."

The bottom drops out of my world because why were we so stupid? Kissing Alessandro outside where anyone could see us and now I know exactly why my brother is calling me back.

Malik starts walking at a brisker pace and I have no option but to follow him but it's not me I'm worried about, and I hope he hasn't already 'spoken' to Alessandro.

21

ANGELO

I am wound up so tight I almost can't breathe. Fucking idiot. He went against my orders and did the one thing I expressly forbid him to.

As he heads into the room and throws his rucksack on the floor, I say from my seat, "I've had a delivery."

I'm not sure how I keep my voice even and controlled because all I see when I look at Alessandro Majerio is a traitor to everything we have built these past few years.

"I'm guessing this 'delivery' concerns me."

He stares at me with a hard expression, and I toss the note I received this morning toward him and watch as he unfolds it and stares at it with a sigh of resignation.

"Who sent it?"

"A coward. Someone who wants to cause trouble, someone with a grudge against us. The list is fucking endless."

I lean forward and stare at him with a warning of what's coming. "That doesn't matter. What does is that you compromised my sister's safety because of what you wanted."

To his credit, he looks as worried as I am and not because of his own safety, because of hers. Then he says roughly, "I won't apologize for caring for your sister."

"I don't want your apology."

I snarl, "I thought I could trust you, Alessandro. I thought you knew how this works."

"I do"

"Then explain why you thought kissing my sister on open ground would help solve her problems because I'm struggling to think that you thought of her once in this."

He stares at me long and hard and growls, "We both know I would never compromise your sister's safety."

"But you did."

I stand and he faces me with a hard look in his eye and snarls, "Maybe I'm not prepared to let her go without a fight. Maybe I've thought of a way out of this shit storm and maybe I want to protect her as much as you do."

"You've only just met! You don't know shit, Alessandro, and this is your dick talking. My one instruction was to stay away from my sister, and I knew you would be a problem the moment I saw the look in your eye when you met her. If you disregard the importance of this, what will you be like when we move this on past graduation? I can't trust you now, and that is our biggest problem."

The door opens and Winter rushes through as if running a race, closely followed by Malik. She looks between us, and I see the relief in her eyes when she sees we're in one piece and says quickly, "What's up?"

I laugh bitterly. "This." I nod to Alessandro, and he tosses her the photograph, and she sighs. "Big deal, so I kissed a guy in college, sentence me to life imprisonment. Oh, I forgot, I'm already heading there."

She faces me and says roughly, "One night only, isn't that your fucking mantra, Angelo. I asked for one kiss, nothing else for one night only. Alessandro tried to refuse. He struggled with that but sometimes the moment catches you and nothing else matters." She looks at Alessandro and smiles ruefully. "I'm sorry I brought this on you. I knew it was wrong, but I don't regret a thing."

Then she looks at me and says sadly, "Angelo, you do far more than kiss. Why is it so different for me?"

"Because of where that kiss could lead!"

I slam my fist down on the table, making her jump a little and I shout, "We all know a kiss just isn't enough! What happens if it leads to something more and God forbid your fucking husband discovers his virgin bride is anything but and slices her neck in revenge because we all know that would happen. How can I keep you safe if you won't take this seriously?"

Winter stares at me in shock and I snarl, "I will say this only once. Stay away from one another for both your sakes. Whoever took this photo knew its significance."

"What are you talking about?" Winter looks horrified and Alessandro looks as if he wants to kill something.

"Kids kiss around campus every minute of the day. So why is this breaking news? Have you asked yourself that?"

I snarl, "The fucker who sent this knew it would cause a rift and set us against one another."

"Has it?"

Malik steps in and says in a calm and deadly tone. "It looks like that from where I'm standing."

We look at him because he is the voice of calm in a raging storm right now.

"Stop fighting among ourselves and work out who stands to gain from delivering this like a coward in the dead of night. Who wants to cause a break in our tight family because I'm guessing it's not a college prank? This is serious and if you stop and think, you'll see we have a far greater problem than your sister sharing a kiss with her brother's friend."

Winter looks worried and Alessandro curses as he snarls, "Have you any idea who it could be?"

Malik faces us with a spark in his eyes and I know this is exactly the kind of thing he loves.

"No but give me twenty-four hours and I'll have a list of names."

"Twelve, and the clock is ticking."

I snap at Winter. "Stay away from Alessandro and don't put him in that position again."

Turning to him, I snarl, "The best way you can keep my sister safe is by keeping your hands to yourself. This isn't about you, me, or Winter. It's about what happens after graduation, and we don't have our plan in place to save her from that."

Winter sits on the couch and sighs heavily and I know my twin and can tell she's thinking about something.

"What?"

"Nothing." She dismisses me and I say to the others. "Leave us."

They move away as I knew they would, leaving us both in the room and taking the seat beside her, I say firmly, "What are you thinking?"

"I'm just wondering if I can somehow escape. Make a

run for it and bury myself somewhere they would never find me."

"Do you think I haven't thought of that already?"

She looks at me in surprise. "Have you?"

"I've thought of everything, Winter and not a lot else. That may buy you some time, but they would find you in the end. You know how it works. This life doesn't let its prisoners go, and we must be smart. Work out a plan that will set us all free and not just for a few weeks or a few months, but forever."

"But how, we're just kids. They have connections worldwide?"

"Then you have your answer. We play the game, and we learn to master it. Just do me a favor and play your part because God help us if you make it to a marital bed and discover it's your death bed instead."

She shivers beside me, and I reach out and grasp her hand, squeezing it tightly. "Trust me, I'm working on it. Just don't take any chances, not now."

"I'm sorry Angelo." She sounds beaten, defeated already and I feel like the biggest bastard alive because above everything I want my sister to smile, to experience freedom and to be like any other kid on campus. Sometimes the impossible is just a decision away and I completely understand why she made that decision last night. One night only, that's all it can be because if that photograph ever made its way home, she would be shipped out within hours and married before the day was done.

22

WINTER

The atmosphere is tense and even Emma notices when she heads home. I feel bad for that because she was just starting to relax and as we all sit in silence at dinner, I can't think of anything else but that photograph. If anything, it makes me mad because who the hell thinks they can play with us like this? I can't look at Alessandro because I feel bad for him and as we finish and I stand to clear the dishes, Flynn says quickly, "I'll help."

I nod and as the others head off in silence, I feel glad it's him because out of everyone, he appears to be finding this mildly amusing.

As I stack the dishes, he says casually, "Things are heating up."

"Are you referring to our stalker, or things with you and Emma?"

He laughs. "Both."

Turning, I look at him in surprise. "Both!"

He looks away and I grab his shoulder and pull him

around to face me. "You can't leave it there. What's happened?"

"Nothing yet."

"You mean, she's booked in her one night with you already."

He throws his head back and laughs. "She told you then."

"Of course."

I look at him with curiosity. "Why are you doing this?"

For a second, his eyes hold a battle of some kind, and it makes my heart beat a little faster. Unpleasant memories are resurfacing, and he looks lost, which tears at my heart.

"Flynn." I whisper his name softly, and he shakes the memory away and shrugs. "Because she deserves to feel special for one night only."

"I'm getting pissed at hearing that sentence, Flynn." Sighing, I start cleaning the dishes. "Why does it have to be one night? I get that you don't want to form attachments, but why only one night?"

"Because of that. When feelings are involved, it becomes something you can't control. Sends you into madness when things change. It's better this way, pleasure without pain. Emma knows the score, and she's happy."

"Are you sure about that?"

"If you don't believe me, ask her yourself. Anyway, we're not the only ones catching attention. What's the score with the beast?"

"One night only, that was the plan. One kiss in the darkness to see what all the fuss was about."

"Are you sure about that?" He grins as I roll my eyes. Then, as I think about it, I shake my head. "I like him, Flynn. God knows why, but there's a connection between us

I know he feels too. This is a fucked-up situation because we can never act on it and see if it faded to nothing like most hook ups do. Maybe I've built it up into something more because of the restrictions on my life."

"You see him as someone who can save you?"

"Of course not." I laugh bitterly, "Nobody can save me but God. We're not strong enough to go against my father, but I'm guessing you know that already."

"Tell me about him."

Staring out of the window, I think about how to sum up a bastard and say sadly, "I'm guessing you know already, probably from first-hand experience. Same fucked-up human with a different face, going by a different name. Everything you hate in life and more besides. A man who has no regard for humanity and no love in his heart. Someone who would kill his own wife because she embarrassed him in public and fucked a politician in the restroom."

Thinking of my mother, I feel nothing but an empty hole in my heart that she punched her way out of many years earlier before she died.

"You know, she was never a mother in the usual way. She gave birth to us and then spent the rest of her miserable life blaming us for putting her through hell. She had a long labor by all accounts and nearly died. We were ignored and brought up by a steady stream of nannies, the longest lasting only two months before they left and never came back. But I always had Angelo, and that was enough for me."

Flynn watches me the whole time as if he understands and then leans against the sink and says softly, "I never had a mother."

"What happened to her?"

He shrugs. "I don't know. The subject was never raised. I think I was a few months old when I was sold to my father."

"Sold!"

I stare at him in horror.

"So I believe." He shrugs as if it's of no consequence. "I only know that because he told me in a fit of rage one day. It made things clearer as to why he treated me so badly because I was his child by dollars, not blood."

"Do you know who she is?"

"No. Maybe I'll find her one day and ask her."

"I'm sorry, Flynn."

He shrugs. "Don't be. You can't be upset over something you never had."

"What will you do when you leave here?"

He laughs bitterly. "I'm expected to learn the business, earn my keep, and protect my father from his many enemies."

"How do you feel about that?"

He laughs out loud. "Winter, my little sis, that I never had, ever heard the saying 'the enemy within.' Well, you're looking at him. Everything I learn is with one aim in mind, slaughtering my father because killing is too kind a word for what I have planned for him."

He stares at me through eyes brimming with madness. "We're all the same in this house, and the demons are circling. Plots, plans and promises are being carefully crafted, and it's only a matter of time before we're free, or dead. Angelo is the most anxious because he has something valuable to lose and if you hate him for being overprotective, know that the rest of us would kill to have someone care for us in the same way. That's why we're a family, Winter, because now there are six of us in this, all willing to die to protect the ones we love. When you've never had love before, when you do, it's like a drug. You will do anything for your next fix knowing it will kill you in the end. That's why we protect ourselves from emotion. Damage limitation is the best form of defense."

He sighs and looks sad for some reason. "I see the pain in Alessandro's face when he looks at you. He can't help his feelings and just knowing your future is causing him to burn inside. Angelo was right to warn you both off and it's not just to protect you. This could fuck Alessandro up far worse than a knife to flesh and if you feel anything for him, you'll respect the boundaries set in place for all our sakes."

Turning, he grins like the mad angel he is, and the kind look in his eyes makes my heart melt. "One thing's for sure, whoever sent that photograph will regret it. Malik's a bastard you would never want to meet on a very dark night. That guy is more fucked-up than me and I thought I held the trophy for that."

Thinking on the dark, brooding, slightly distant Arab, I shiver inside because one look from him is like feeling a thousand knives scraping against your skin, wondering which one will end your life. I know Flynn is right. He gives nothing away and I pity the person set in his sights, whoever they may be.

∼

ONCE I'VE FINISHED the dishes, I head off to my books but can't resist stopping by Emma's study where she sits for most of the night.

I tap gently on the door and expect to find her at her desk. and am surprised when I find it empty.

Heading to her room, I hear the shower and sit on her bed to wait and it's not long before she heads out toweling her hair dry.

She jumps when she sees me and laughs nervously, "You startled me."

"Sorry." I smile and scoot back on the bed and fix her with a curious look. "Are you heading out?"

She blushes a little. "I am."

"Where?" I can only think she has a study date at the library or something with her circle of like-minded friends.

She blushes and I gasp, "Tell me."

Sitting on the bed, she looks worried. "I'm sorry, Winter. I can't think about anything else. Ever since Flynn gave me a choice, it's eaten away at me. You know, he met me from class today. Me, the girl nobody sees and spends her time watching others get all the attention."

"That was nice." I smile and I'm pleased for her in a weird way because just the light dancing in her eyes tells me she's loving every second of this. She says almost dreamily, "He walked with me to my next class and carried my bag. He was funny and sweet and nothing like I imagined. I felt like a queen–his queen and it was good to be looked at differently, like I was someone who counted for just a brief moment."

"I'm pleased for you, Emma." I smile because seeing her happy makes me happy but I'm still worried and say tentatively, "But how will you feel when he doesn't look at you the next day because it could happen you know?"

I'm surprised when she laughs and says like she's comforting a child, "I'm ok with that. I just want to feel special, and he has promised to make it a night I will never forget. I just want that experience so I can shake this longing I feel that's burning me from the inside. I want to know what's so great about that secret I've never had the opportunity to learn and then I can go back to the books and do what I came here for. One night only is all I want, and I'm absolutely sure about that."

I'm worried for my friend because I'm not sure she's thinking this through, and she shrugs. "It's a risk I'm willing to take. Wish me luck."

As I smile, I feel a lot of envy toward Emma. At least she will have a nice memory to look back on. She's making her own decisions on her own terms, and I wish I had that luxury. Just thinking about my first time makes me sad because I'll never feel that giddiness that's apparent in her eyes. My own experience is bound to be hard to deal with because the man who makes it happen is likely to be even more of a bastard than my father who won't waste this opportunity to merge our family with a more powerful one. Then the man I'm promised to will use me like a possession with none of the love I crave.

23

ANGELO

It's as if there's a dark cloud of depression surrounding me as I move around Rockwell Academy like an avenging angel. I suspect everyone, and anyone that catches my eye is frowned upon as I figure out whether they could be the person responsible for that photograph.

Apparently, Miss. English has decided she's pissed at being ignored and when the bell goes, says sharply, "Angelo, please stay behind."

There is none of the interest that statement usually brings with it because I'm not in the mood for her today and even Alessandro doesn't hang back, and I'm not surprised. He's so wrapped up in feelings for my sister it should annoy me, but I just feel sadness for my friend who I know hasn't had much love in his life, like us all really. At least I have my sister, but my friends have no one.

I'm not surprised they crave Winter's attention and not only in a sexual way. She's a soft breath of fresh air in an atmosphere that's deepening by the second. An ominous promise of a dark life that we will struggle to survive.

Winter, and Emma to a degree, bring a different dynamic to the house, showing us how different life could be if we were allowed to choose. Maybe we are luckier than Winter because at least we get to set the tone in our relationships, but marriage for power doesn't give us many choices. It's why our fathers fuck around so much because their own marriages leave them cold.

Miss. English is looking like bubble-gum wrapped in cotton candy and for once it's something I need right now. Not the hard fuck against the wall of the stationery closet, but someone to hold and wrap me in comfort. Dangerous ground that could shift and take me under, so I fix a scowl on my face and wait for what she has in mind.

The door closes, and she perches on the edge of the desk, her skirt riding high enough to see she's ready to go, and she pouts prettily. "You've been avoiding me."

"In your mind." I yawn and she says sadly, "Honey, don't shut me out. You know, Principal Stoner is getting weary of the stories that reach his office. Two girls terrorized at one of your parties who left minus their hair one night. Whispered tales of gambling and one-night stands." She shakes her head. "It's not behavior that can be ignored much longer."

I shrug. "Why don't you add fucking a teacher to that list and see what he does then?"

Her eyes flash and she leans forward, revealing her soft curves which make me hard despite myself. "Don't you worry about me, baby. I can handle my own shit, but I'm worried about you. Things are heating up and for your own sake you need to tone it down a bit before you end up out on your ass before graduation."

"Lecture over, Miss. English." I raise my eyes and throw

her the usual fuck off look that I direct to most of the teachers in this school. "Is there anything else, or can I head to lunch? I'm rather hungry as it happens and have some freshmen to chew the fucking heads off, hair and all."

She laughs softly. "There he is, my big, bad boy. You know, I've been thinking."

I shrug. "It happens sometimes."

Easing off the desk, she approaches me and leans down, her soft sweet breath grazing my ear as she whispers, "Meet me at my house later tonight. You know the one. I'll leave the back door open, and we can continue this discussion then. I'll make it worth your while, and it may just settle your anger–a little."

I'm surprised at the invitation because this is a first. Miss. English shares her house with Miss. Potts, one of the phys ed teachers, and by all accounts she has a thing for Miss. English herself.

"Will you be alone?" I'm mildly curious, and she nods. "Miss. Potts has been called home to a family emergency and won't be back for a few days. It's an opportunity I don't want to waste and who better to keep me company than my favorite student. We could, um, study hard with no interruptions. What do you say?"

"I say nothing."

I shift from my seat and as I stand, I feel an overwhelming longing to pull her close and bury my face in her sweet tits and just stay there. I am desperate for affection, love even, but know it's not something I can allow. Maybe Miss. English will offer me something I can't take from another, so I push back and leave without another word, knowing where I'll be heading later because a night buried deep in a soft pussy with no repercussions sounds extremely good right now.

MALIK IS WAITING and as we move toward the house to grab lunch, I say in a low voice, "You got anything yet?"

I don't know how he does it, but Malik can discover just about anything within a matter of hours, and part of me wonders if he's bugged the whole academy. He's always been a master at electronics and even installed a camera in the principal's office to gather intel on him. Something we could use against him if the occasion arose, but that fucker is so boring he does nothing but work. Admirable, really, but extremely unhelpful. At least it gave us the heads up on Winter which made my blood boil when I discovered my father had sent her here. I still can't work out why? We only have a few months before graduation. Why uproot her from Glendale Academy and start her somewhere new with such a short time left?

Malik says in his twisted accent, "The cameras picked up a figure dressed in black, disguised by a face mask, around 4 am. They slipped the note under the door and ran away."

"Male, female?"

"Too difficult to tell. Whoever it was made themselves a shadow."

"The mask?"

I stare at him thoughtfully. "What was it?"

"An animal of some kind."

"You've got that right."

My blood boils when I think of this person messing

with us and I long to get my hands on them and rip the truth from them with the most horrific force. It's been a while since I've had that pleasure. School doesn't offer many opportunities to hone the particular skills we'll need in our lives. It's why Alessandro and Ivan knock chunks out of each other for the practice. Malik likes to practice mind manipulation, usually with a willing girl under him and I often wonder what games he thinks up because the fear in many of his casual fuck's eyes when they see him coming, tells me he's got some weird shit he likes to play behind closed doors.

Then there's Flynn, our very own fallen angel, who, out of all of us, loves a different kind of project; a more noble one that rips the hearts out of every girl he fucks because he treats them so well and then leaves them crying for what they can never have. A different kind of game that always ends in tears, which is why I'm worried about Winter's friend Emma, because she fits the usual profile of his victims, and we will have to deal with the consequences of that.

Sighing, I say moodily, "What's the plan?"

"I've set up surveillance and dropped a whisper in the relevant ears around campus. If they strike again or speak of it, I should hear back within a few minutes. Whoever they are will be unmasked if they make another move, so we sit tight and wait for that to happen."

"Do you think it will?" I'm not so sure and he laughs, "Why go to all that trouble for one photograph? I'm guessing there's way more to it than that and probably involves your sister's placement here."

"What are you thinking?" It always amazes me how Malik's mind works, and it *always* appears to be working because like me, he's already decided Winter's arrival concerns more than just passing her exams and I'm keen to know what he thinks about that.

"I'm guessing this is part of your father's plan for her future. She's either being set up, or we are?"

Just thinking of my father and his mind games tells me Malik's spot on and I sigh heavily. "I'm guessing you're right. But why? I mean, Winter's only function in his life is to connect with someone powerful, someone he chooses."

"Then we need to make a list and decide who that's likely to be. Remember, my friend, we are all here at the same place and maybe that has something to do with this. Perhaps your father is keen to use Winter to get to one of us. We just need to work out which one he has set his sights on."

"Do you think it's that easy?"

I laugh bitterly. "I wish that was the case. That he wants her to marry one of you to join our families, but my father's not so kind. I'm guessing Winter's future husband is ancient and all powerful. Someone needing a wife, perhaps. Someone who is currently without one. Maybe we should look at any possible candidates for that and narrow down the field because if I know my father, Winter is here to cause trouble and I'm guessing that's designed to break our friendship apart."

"Then he would be doing a good job already."

Malik sounds casual, but I know his mind is probably racing with possibilities and I nod. "Alessandro."

He says nothing and I think about what has happened already and say darkly, "Then he hasn't realized how deep our ties run because even though I want to kill Alessandro right now, I still love him like the brother he is. If anything,

I wish it was that easy and that my father has marriage in mind with him, but it's more likely he wants to ruin our friendship and leave me with no friends to count on."

As the penny drops, we stare at one another with a moment of enlightenment and my stomach churns when I think of my father plotting to rip us apart and set us against one another. He knew I wouldn't tolerate Winter living apart from me on campus, and he knows how protective I am of her. He placed the ticking bomb right inside the fortress and is waiting for her to blow us apart.

Malik says with a sigh. "I'm sorry my friend, as always, life's a bitch. You need to push aside your anger and work out who's helping him because I'm guessing the person who delivered that photograph did it under your father's instruction. If I'm right, then more will follow if he, or she, reports back and tell him nothing has changed. This could be the start of something that will test us more than any final exam, but this time we'll be waiting and use it to our advantage."

We reach the house and I shoot him a look that is reflected right back at me, and we nod as if we've just signed a declaration of war and for some reason, I feel a shiver of expectation pass through me because this is what I love, what I thrive on and what feeds the hunger within me. Games of the most destructive kind that I plan on winning in the end and if my father is messing with us, it just feeds the obsession I have to end his miserable life, in a cold and callous way.

24

WINTER

I'm surprised when Claudia calls out when I leave science. "Winter, wait up."

Spinning around, I smile as she races toward me, looking flushed. "Hey, sorry, I just wanted to catch your attention."

We start walking toward the canteen and she sighs. "Listen, I've been meaning to ask if you fancied hanging out one night."

"Me?" I'm surprised because Claudia is one of the popular girls and dates the most popular guys. Rumor has it she's back with her ex, Joey and probably has a million other girls all wanting to stand by her side, so a little of her magic rubs off on them.

"Listen, there's a party at Max's house this evening. Why don't you meet me there?"

"I'm not..." She stops and looks disappointed. "Please don't say no. I'd really like us to be friends and kind of think you need a bit of fun in your life. It can't be easy for you living in that house and, well, I'd like to help."

"Why? I mean, it's really kind of you, but I'm sure you don't need another friend."

She looks a little hurt, which makes me feel bad, and she sighs. "Listen, word is, you're nothing like your brother or his friends. Most people like you and feel bad that you're missing out on things by association. The fact you stood up to Eden and Brianna when they attacked me makes me owe you big time. I just want to be your friend because one kind act deserves another. Come and see what life at Rockwell Academy is really like. I promise you, it's nothing more than that."

She smiles and looks so hopeful, it makes me smile and I feel as if a huge cloud of tension leaves me because she's offering me something I've always wanted. Acceptance, friendship and a night of freedom and who wouldn't be interested in that, so I smile. "Then thanks, I'd love to come."

She exhales with relief. "Thank God. I really thought you'd say no."

"Why?"

"Because of your brother. He doesn't mix with the rest of us, and I thought you'd be the same."

"He has parties; you've been there. I suppose that's his idea of mixing."

She laughs. "Yes, he does throw a good party and I suppose the attraction is curiosity for the most part."

"I get that." I laugh because Angelo has never had a problem attracting attention and I'm guessing it's no different here.

Claudia sighs. "Every girl loves a bad boy, and he has that nailed good and proper. You know, he focused his attention on me one night and it was a powerful thing."

"I kind of guessed." I wonder if she's just using me to get close to him and my heart sinks. "Look, maybe I'll bail tonight. I've got lots of assignments due and..."

"I'm sorry, Winter. I hope you don't think I invited you because of him."

She looks troubled. "That's not what the invitation was about. I really do want to thank you for stepping in and helping me; nothing more than that. Please say you'll come."

Relaxing a little, I nod. "Can I bring Emma?"

She looks surprised. "Um, of course, but well, do you think she'll come? It's just that she usually keeps herself locked away studying."

Thinking about my friend, I wonder if she'll turn me down because she hates parties, especially ones with the more popular students and I shrug. "I'll see what she thinks."

We reach the canteen, which is buzzing, and I see her wave to a table filled with her friends. "Come and meet the gang. They'll love you, honey, so don't be shy."

I have no choice but follow and notice several curious glances in our direction as I walk beside her.

Claudia's friends are the kind of students everyone wants to be seen with. Max, the captain of the team and his three friends are probably the most desired guys on campus, not just because of their amazing looks and bodies, legendary parties and supposed wealth but because they're mainly good guys who like to have fun.

I see Baron watching me and shiver when I stare into his dark eyes. He is the exception to the rule and is an ominous presence in a house filled with sunshine. He fits in more with Angelo's own group of friends and yet there's something about him that feels like home. I stare at Max, the man everyone orbits hoping for one moment of his attention, and he smiles as I approach. "Hey, a fresh face, take a seat and tell us all your secrets."

Feeling all eyes on me makes me uncomfortable because I hate being the center of attention and always have, so I smile shyly and squash myself beside Claudia and Baron, who shifts up a little to give us more space.

I can feel Baron tense beside me and wonder why and as Max's attention is taken by an attractive girl to his side, Baron whispers, "You ok?"

"I think so."

He says thoughtfully, "What's the score with Claudia? I never had you down as friends."

"Neither did I?" Raising my eyes, I throw him a look, and he grins. "I see. Interesting."

"She's invited me to a party at your house tonight. Do you think I should come?"

"Why not." He shrugs. "I'll be there and have your back. Enjoy yourself."

"If only it was that easy." I laugh and he nods with a hint of sympathy. "You can try at least; maybe it's what you need."

"You know Baron..." I grin. "I think you're right. Maybe I will see what happens. I'm pretty sure I deserve some fun and I expect Angelo won't be around to spoil it, so why not. I'll see you there."

He nods and the spark in his eyes tells me he's interested to see what happens, telling me he's exactly like my brother. They like living on the edge and provoking the unexpected and, for some reason, I feel excited about what may happen later tonight. Maybe this is the night

Winter gets to experience something new. I certainly hope so because my night of freedom is a long time coming.

Later, after school, I head straight to Emma's room because I am burning with curiosity about her 'date' last night. She wasn't back when I made it to bed, and I was worried when she had left already when I woke up. Then again, maybe she never made it home, or spent the night in a different room. Who knows, but I need to make that my priority and head straight to her room?

"Emma."

She looks up from her desk where she's already hitting the books and smiles, and the tension leaves me in a big wave of relief. She seems ok, so that's a good thing at least and I grab a seat on the couch in her huge study room and smile. "So."

"What?" she grins impishly and if anything looks quite smug and I am burning with curiosity. "Your night? What happened?"

"If you are referring to the best night of my life, then quite a lot happened."

She looks so animated it makes me smile and I watch as she gets up and closes the door before sitting beside me on the couch.

"Where do I start?" She giggles and just hearing it settles my heart and I wait to hear all the gory details.

"We went to the cinema to see that new horror movie everyone's talking about."

"You like that kind of thing?" I'm surprised because Emma seems scared of her own shadow half the time.

"It's not my usual preference but Flynn told me it was a

night of experiencing new things and promised to hold my hand and protect me."

She sighs and can't stop the shit-eating grin on her face and whispers, "It was amazing. We saw some kids from college who couldn't believe who I was with. I felt so important and like the luckiest girl on the planet. I've heard them all talking, and Flynn is quite a legend around campus. One night with him ruins a girl for anyone else–so I'm told, anyway."

I feel quite jealous and say eagerly, "Then what happened?"

"Well, we made out a bit in the cinema, the darkness making me more comfortable about it and it was amazing. He's such a good kisser, not that I have anything to compare it to and really made me feel as if he wanted me. He was soft, gentle and romantic and I suppose it was inevitable we ended up in his bed."

"You did what?"

My jaw drops and she giggles again.

"After the movie, we grabbed pizza, and it felt so natural despite how scary he is. He has this way about him of freezing everyone out and focused his attention firmly on me. It was quite a lot to handle, especially because nobody ever has before, and he just kept on paying me compliments and telling me how beautiful I am."

She blushes and looks a little sad and whispers, "I know he's wrong, but last night I believed it myself. He made me feel beautiful. Like the bad skin and glasses were a serious turn on. The fact I'm overweight with zero dress sense didn't seem to matter to him and he couldn't tear his eyes from mine and kept stroking my hair, saying it was his favorite color, which almost made me believe he was genuine."

"Maybe he is. Perhaps you're his idea of the perfect woman and why wouldn't you be?"

I feel bad for her because a lifetime of dismissive comments and people ignoring you can harm a person's soul and make them believe they're not worthy of love. Thinking of Flynn and his apparent interest in my friend makes me wonder about his story. I do believe he's genuine. Nobody could fabricate this for as long as he has. I've seen the way he looks at her, sad, wistful even, as if she provokes a memory that he cherishes yet kills him inside. Part of me wonders if she reminds him of someone and decide to ask Angelo about his story when he gets back this evening.

She carries on, saying dreamily, "I almost never went through with it. When we got to his room, I had a panic attack. I suppose the thought of him seeing me naked was the first trigger and then the thought of actually, well, you know, made me doubt my own mind."

"I'm sorry, Emma." Reaching for her hand, I squeeze it gently and she shrugs. "Flynn made the doubts disappear. He held me and rocked me gently, like a baby. He wiped my tears away and then kissed me softly. He made me feel something so amazing, I wanted to explore it further and when he took me to bed, it was because it was something we both wanted."

"And was it?" I am hanging onto every word because I'm fascinated by her story. It sounds so romantic it makes my own heart ache for the same and she nods. "It was amazing. *He* was so amazing, I actually cried tears of happiness. He worked my body like a master and made it experience things I never thought it could do. I was a different person with him, Winter. Reborn and remolded into a much better version of myself. I feel so powerful now because the pleasure I gave him was not fabricated. It was real and afterward he held me in his arms as if he never wanted to let me go. It was the best experience of my life, and I don't regret a thing."

"What happens next?" I'm worried about that, and she shrugs. "We get on with our lives as friends."

"And you're happy about that?" I'm not sure I would be, and she nods. "Perfectly happy. I knew it was a onetime thing; he made that very clear. To be honest, I need to work hard for my finals, and it's helped focus my mind. He removed all the anxiety about something that is so beautiful I don't know what I was worried about, and I feel—well, I feel like a woman instead of a frightened girl and know that I can walk out of Rockwell and take on life on my terms. 'One night only' he said, and that's fine by me because now I know I'm just like the rest of the girls here, and Flynn has given me the greatest gift a girl could receive. He took my virginity and made it so special it will always be the happiest of memories with none of the pain that goes with a relationship and the pain of a breakup. I'm happy about that, strange as it seems, and I just wish you could have the same memory as I do."

"With Flynn?" I laugh and she shakes her head. "Probably not, but I can recommend it." She winks and sighs with satisfaction. "But I know of someone else you'd probably prefer, and I wish you had the freedom to see where that leads."

She looks at her watch and says guiltily, "Sorry, I have a date at the library with my study group. I'm catching a takeout with them, so maybe some other time."

"That's fine, although…"

"What?"

"I came to ask you to a party next door. Claudia invited us both and it would mean a lot if you came too."

The old Emma would have a ready-made excuse on her lips, but the new, confident Emma just smiles brightly. "Great, I'm up for that. Just let me study hard first so I can dip out for a couple of hours and not feel guilty."

She grins as she rushes to grab her things and I'm left wondering at attraction and just how powerful that can be.

As I head to my room, I feel so jealous of my friend because at least she's had something so special it can never be taken away from her. If only I was half as lucky and, with a sigh, I head to my own pile of books and wonder if it's even worth my time because there's no way in hell my education is going to play any part in my future and that sucks—big time.

25

ANGELO

We eat as a family, but this time Emma is missing. Winter told me she's eating with friends at the library, and I wonder if that has anything to do with Flynn, who doesn't look as if he gives a fuck as he stares at his food with an odd expression.

"What's up?" Alessandro nudges him. "You're looking as if someone poisoned your food. You finally catching feelings or something?" He nods toward Emma's empty chair and Flynn stares at him with his usual dead expression. "As if that will ever happen."

"What then?"

My senses are on high alert because Flynn is the monster under most people's beds, mine included, and it's not unheard of to wake up and find him sitting in the corner of the room in the dark shadows watching us sleep. We've all had that particular pleasure, and it scares the shit out of us.

"Just thinking about graduation."

The atmosphere in the room thickens with a sense of

damnation as he refers to the storm approaching for every last one of us and I say sharply, "Remain focused."

We've spoken about that day almost as long as we've been living in this house and the fact it's almost upon us is creating a sense of urgency because we're still searching for the magic ingredient to set us all free.

Ivan yawns. "Same. I'm not even getting my usual pleasure from beating the fuck out of the beast here?"

Alessandro laughs darkly. "In your dreams, you fucking pussy, a senior would cause more damage than you."

"Fancy talking about that in the ring?"

"If you like. There's nothing else to do."

His words sound empty and cold, and I don't miss the way he completely refuses to look at Winter, who is chewing her food with a thoughtful expression.

"What about you, sis? What's your plan tonight?"

I need to know because my own involves being buried balls deep in Miss. English, and she shrugs. "Claudia invited me and Emma to the house next door. There's a party."

The tense silence reveals we're of the same mind and I flick my eyes at Malik, who leans back and only his gleaming eyes tell me he's excited about that. We share a look and whereas I would ordinarily forbid her from attending, especially with a masked stalker out there, I know this could be an opportunity too good to miss.

I nod to him, and he grins as he picks up his fork and starts shoveling his food down, seemingly in a better mood because of it.

"Be careful and enjoy yourself."

Alessandro looks at me sharply and I can tell I've surprised, if not angered him and Ivan laughs as he nudges his friend. "I'd better watch myself tonight. Someone's feeling pissed."

"Fuck you, Ivan. I'll pound your ass and walk away, still hungry for a proper fight."

Flynn yawns. "I'm heading out."

Malik looks as concerned as I do because this is not unusual. Once Flynn has finished with his latest project, he goes rogue for a few days, usually in town. It's almost as if he needs the solitude to get his head back in the right space. I instructed Malik to follow him a few times to check on him, but Flynn is a clever bastard and managed to give him the slip every time and rocked up a few days later with none of the murderous rage in his eyes that he left with. This is a problem I don't want tonight because I need all eyes on that party and this house because I'm guessing whoever is watching us and taking an interest in my sister could use this opportunity to cause more trouble.

Winter pushes back her chair and grabs her plate, heading to the sink, and I say evenly, "Leave it. We'll clean up tonight."

Her blinding smile pains me more than she knows because the thought of not seeing her smile in her future reminds me the sand timer is almost out.

"Thanks. I'll head to my room and finish my assignment. Emma's back soon, and we'll head next door for a couple of hours."

We watch her leave and only when we hear the door slam upstairs do I say darkly, "We need to make sure she's safe."

Alessandro nods. "I thought the same. Why are you letting her go to one of Max's parties? You know every fucker on campus will want a piece of her. She's fresh meat and probably the best-looking girl here."

I look at him sharply and to his credit, he just stares me down and I say tightly, "Because we need this person to make another move and if we have eyes on her, we're more likely to catch them."

I look at Flynn. "You up for that?"

The dark rage swirling in his eyes makes me wonder if he's in the right head space for this because Flynn is one breath from madness most days and I know it has everything to do with his upbringing. He never speaks of it, but he's been damaged more than the rest of us put together and really should see a shrink about that.

"I'll watch."

I breathe a sigh of relief because if I can focus his mind on something, it may give him a place to hide until the storm in his head passes and I look across at Malik. "What about you?"

"I'll stay here and observe another way."

He looks excited about that and I'm guessing he's referring to the surveillance he has set up around the place, which means we have eyes on the house in case anyone decides to visit without asking.

Ivan cracks his knuckles. "I'll act as security. Baron mentioned the party, so I may as well take advantage of that."

Alessandro rolls his eyes. "The only thing you'll see is the fucking wall as you hammer some fucking cheerleader to it."

Ivan grins and shrugs. "It passes the time."

Of all of us, I think Ivan is cut out for this life the most. He appears to thrive on conflict, pain and retribution and the fact he's been trained in every martial art ever invented has made him a killing machine of the most dangerous kind. Only Alessandro can match him, and he struggles sometimes, but Ivan is using the time to teach his friend everything he knows, because Alessandro wants to fight his way out of the mafia if needed. His own father distanced himself from his true birth right in Sicily, and Alessandro's grandfather is one of the most feared and respected mafia Dons in the world. I know it worries him a lot because word is, his father bargained his own place at the head of the family for his son and Alessandro could be shipped off to Sicily as soon as the graduation ceremony is done and there is nothing he can do about that.

"I'll keep watch outside." He sighs. "I could use the thinking time."

I look at him sharply because I know he's struggling, and not just with his feelings for my sister. You could cut the atmosphere with a knife when they're in the same room and I know this is a pressurized situation that I should be concerned about. If anything, I'm surprised that he caught feelings so quickly. He's not one for looking at a girl twice, let alone longing after them like a lovesick fool. Then there's my sister, asking him to kiss her when she knows the consequences of that. I'm not sure she can be trusted now, which is why I need her always watched, to protect her from herself.

Malik says suddenly, "What about you, Angelo?"

Thinking of Miss. English, I wonder if my visit should be postponed.

"I've had an invitation to study history at the teacher's house."

The guys laugh out loud, and it pricks the bubble of

tension that's hanging in the air. Ivan growls, "Fuck me, I'd love a night like that." Malik grins. "Wouldn't we all, you lucky bastard."

Thinking of our accommodating teacher, I grin because a night of sex with her is like being given a hall pass to do anything I like. No boundaries and no repercussions and I'm guessing she could teach me a few things I've never even heard of.

"I'm not sure it's a good idea."

"The fuck it is." Ivan laughs out loud. "Maybe you could pump her for information."

Malik rolls his eyes. "Savage."

Ivan grins and his eyes flash with a wickedness that almost makes me laugh. Savage is the perfect way to describe our Russian friend because his fists enjoy a full workout most nights. When he's not practicing on Alessandro, he's heading to the underground fight club in town to fight for money and always comes back richer for it.

Now we all have our jobs to do, I feel bad that I'm the one who gets a night off for once and say with a sigh. "Well, I'm not going. It's not a good time."

Malik shakes his head. "It's the perfect time."

"Why?"

"Because if someone is watching, they'll see you leave, and it may make them bolder. If it's you they're after, and we're not certain of that, this could be their chance to make a move. We have eyes on Winter, and you will have your eyes on our decidedly immoral teacher and the rest of us will be watching. It's perfect."

I can see the sense in that and feel like the luckiest one here as I smile with a smugness that doesn't go unnoticed. "Lucky bastard." Alessandro growls and I laugh out loud.

"What's the matter beast man, you thinking of sharing again?"

The look of distaste on his face makes the others laugh out loud and, as the atmosphere lightens, I take a deep breath of relief. Tonight could throw up some answers we need to make our plan and I hope whoever is out there comes in with all guns blazing because knowing my friends, they will take great delight in bringing them down.

26

WINTER

The house next door is so different from ours. As we walk up the path, loud music greets us, and it appears that every light is on in the place. Laughter and loud voices tell me it's packed already, and couples are already making out against the painted wall, making me slightly nervous. This is what I imagined college parties to look like, and Emma edges a little closer.

"Are you ok?" I'm still a little concerned for my friend because even though she has grown in confidence, she's still not used to being in places like this and would still be happier locked in the library with her books.

"I'm fine, excited really."

She smiles and I think how pretty she's looking tonight. Her hair is freshly washed and gleams as the artificial light catches it, and she has tried extra hard with her make-up which covers her acne almost entirely. She's ditched the glasses for contacts and is wearing a top that enhances her generous cleavage and well-cut jeans that complement her curves rather than draw attention to her size. In fact, I don't think I've ever seen Emma looks so amazing and I credit Flynn with that. He's given her confidence, which is the best gift a person can get, and it's made a huge difference. In fact, she's almost unrecognizable from the girl I first met, and I see the respectful glances thrown her way as we pass through the crowds. Word has got out about the company she keeps, and I love the mixture of envy and fascination she now enjoys.

I feel a little nervous because for the first time we're away from the watchful eyes of my brother and his friends and even though Baron is here, he is nowhere near as intense as the guys we live with.

Claudia shrieks when she sees us coming and waves furiously from an open doorway in the corner of the room.

"Winter, over here."

We head her way, and she rushes up and hugs me hard before smiling at Emma. "Glad you made it. Come and grab a drink."

She leads us into the large modern kitchen, and I stare in awe at how amazing this room is. It appears they have every modern convenience going and the polished marble counters don't fit with the usual basic functions of a college kitchen. Not for the first time, I wonder about Max Augustus and his friends. Duke, Gabriel and Baron all make a tight-knit group that are the envy of every kid in Rockwell Academy. Seriously loaded and totally gorgeous, they don't have a regular girl between them, much like the sinister house next door. However, unlike our house of battered souls, this one is light and drama free and I smile as Claudia leans in and whispers, 'There are quite a few guys here with you in their sights tonight. Joey told me half the team is stoked you're here, especially without your brother keeping watch. Is there anyone you fancy getting to know? I could play cupid if you like."

I doubt she's wrong because several pairs of eyes are glancing our way with interest, and I feel a little nervous yet excited about that.

"No, I'm good, thanks. Maybe just see what happens."

She nods. "Well, just shout if you do."

The music changes and she squeals, "I love this song, come and dance."

She's like an over eager puppy as she grabs my hand and pulls me outside into the yard, decorated with strings of fairy lights and a place to dance. Emma shakes her head as I make to pull her with me and laughs. "I'm fine here watching, thanks."

I feel bad as I'm swallowed up in the crowd and as Claudia starts dancing madly, I'm caught up in the excitement of it all and let myself go for once. In fact, I don't think I've ever felt so free in my life and as I dance under the blackened sky, the stars twinkling like diamonds looking down on me, I feel giddy with a moment of normality that's been a long time coming.

Claudia's boyfriend, Joey, muscles his way in and grabs her, almost devouring her neck as she grinds against him, leaving me on the edge dancing alone. I don't care about that because this is so liberating and as I dance, I allow myself to believe in the impossible for once in my life.

I watch out for Emma and see her laughing at something a guy is whispering in her ear, and I look at him with interest. He seems nice and genuine and whatever he's saying makes her laugh out loud. Watching her from a distance, she looks more at home here than I ever thought she'd be, and I feel so happy for her. Maybe sex does that for a girl. Takes away the mystery surrounding it and sets you free to explore life without fear. Extinguish that feeling when your mind is clouded with mystery and whispered tales of an act that sounds frightening and wrong on every level.

A hand slips around my waist and startles me and I stare up at a guy who must be over six feet tall and just as wide. Nowhere near as big as Ivan or Alessandro but a lot less scary.

He looks at me with amusement. "Hey pretty lady, you've been allowed out to play for once. Fancy dancing with me, I don't bite."

Feeling a little on edge, I don't think I'm ready for this and step back and smile nervously, "I'm, um, good thanks."

He presses in. "Don't be like that. I don't bite, not unless you want me to."

He pulls me closer and just feeling his hand around my waist makes me panic a little and then, like a knight in shining armor, I hear a low voice say darkly, "Move on, Jace."

His hand drops immediately, and he backs off. 'Sorry man, I didn't know she was with you. I apologize."

I've never seen anyone back off so fast and look at Baron with a mixture of relief and curiosity. He grins and half bows. "At your service."

"Idiot." I grin as he nods toward the side where a couple of high stools are leaning against a high table. "Time out?"

I nod, following him and sitting down with relief.

"Thanks. Who was that guy?"

"Jace Richards. Wide receiver and asshole of the most annoying kind. Hits on every fresh face going, thinking he's irresistible. I've done you a favor there, actually I've probably done him one because he wouldn't have been able to resist hitting on you, which could have cost him his future career."

"It's not that bad." I laugh, but we both know how bad it really is. Baron's right, one word of any guy hitting on me reaching Angelo's ears would cause trouble for whoever dared to try.

"I'm surprised you're here."

"Why?"

He pushes a glass of water toward me. "Angelo's a protective bastard who would hate seeing you hit on by every jock on campus. It must suck."

"He means well." I sip the water and wish I could drink a beer at least, but it appears Baron has decided I'm not to be trusted, which makes me angry. He sips his own beer and places it on the table, and I swoop in and grab it before he can blink. Chugging it down, I drain the bottle. What was left anyway and stare at him defiantly as he laughs.

"Point well made."

I grin. "I could use another."

"Nice try."

He appears amused, and I look at him with interest. "Where are you from, Baron?"

He shrugs. "All over. Mainly New York, I like it there."

"Not that far from us in Boston. I wish I could say we could meet up after graduation, but I doubt that will happen."

Once again, my future resurfaces and reminds me of how shit my life is, and Baron shrugs. "Never say never, Winter. I'm a great believer that you make your own luck in life and remember what I said to you. Bide your time and use it wisely. Search out weakness and exploit it. Craft your own future with the tools and materials you've got and don't be a victim. You're a smart girl, you'll work it out."

"You know, Baron..." I feel a warmth spreading through me that's not just down to the beer. "I like hanging with you. You make me feel good about things, which isn't easy."

He nods as he scans the room. "I like you too and if you ever need any help, you know where I am."

I feel the attention on us and see a group of girls openly staring at Baron and I nod my head toward them. "You have a fan club, it seems."

He looks across with a blank expression. "They're probably pissed I'm with you."

"Is one of them your girl?" I'm curious because I've never heard any gossip regarding Baron about who keeps him company and he shakes his head. "I don't do relationships, Winter. Like your brother and his friends, there's no point because once I leave Rockwell Academy, I have a particular future lined up for me. We all do."

I know he's referring to his own group of friends as well as mine and I say with curiosity, "What will you do?"

"Business." He smiles. "Big business that requires a clear head, and no strings attached. College is good for many things, but I'm not intending on forming a relationship with anybody here unless it benefits my future."

"That's cold."

"So is life."

Emma heads across with the guy she's been speaking to. "Hey, Winter, this is Corey. He's in my math class."

I smile at the rather nervous guy who is looking as if he wants to be somewhere else entirely and I expect it's because Baron is like the lord of darkness, watching him with a hooded expression.

"Hi, Corey." I smile and he nods nervously as Emma says lightly, "We're going to grab a drink. Can I fetch you one?"

I flash Baron a determined look and say quickly, "I'll come with you."

Jumping down, I say over my shoulder, "Thanks for the chat, Baron. Catch you later."

He nods and the slight smirk on his face makes me smile. For some reason, I like the rather sinister guy who sits on the side-lines of our group looking in and always seems to be there for me when I need him most. However, I also need to let loose for one night and I intend to make the most of every hour of freedom I've got.

27

ANGELO

The place is in darkness, and I move stealthily toward Miss. English's house on the other side of campus. The teachers live in a block hidden by trees and Miss. English and Miss. Potts share the one right on the edge near the forest. The huge chain-link fence keeps the outside where it belongs and as I move in the shadows, I anticipate a night of sin.

This is a long time coming because a fuck against the wall isn't cutting it anymore and I need a good solid fuck to clear my mind, which is why I was keen to keep our appointment.

We both know what this is, and it suits me just fine. No strings sex with a sexy woman a few years older than me.

As I reach the back door, it opens before I raise my hand to knock, and I stare at a woman who would star in most men's fantasies.

She's wearing a tight top that barely covers her generous tits and the shortest skirt that doesn't even deserve the description. Her hungry eyes lure me inside and she whispers huskily, "I'm glad you made it."

Nodding, I stroll inside and look at a basic house with no homey touches, and that surprises me a little. I always had her down as a lover of fancy things and she sees my expression and laughs. "This place is a dog, isn't it? Miss. Potts doesn't like clutter and God forbid I brought a cushion into her sterile space. That woman's a machine, it's not healthy.

She laughs. "My room's through there and way more comfortable."

She smiles suggestively. "I've got some drinks cooling in there. Follow me."

I watch her ass sway from side to side as she leads the way and feel my cock stirring as it anticipates being let loose in the garden of depravity tonight.

I laugh softly when I see Miss. English's room and it's exactly as I imagined it.

Barbie's bedroom, dressed in pink and white, with fur throws on the bed and fluffy rugs on the floor. Fairy lights and cuteness that would be any man's worst nightmare with cuddly animals on shelves and mirrors on the wall.

"How old are you?" I shake my head and laugh, and she grins, tossing me a beer from a cooler by the bed. "Don't you like it?"

She shifts her legs under her on the bed and leans back against the many pillows crowding the space.

"I don't dislike it."

She is gazing at me with a hunger that I share, and I take a swig of cold beer and watch her do the same, her eyes never leaving mine for a second.

Slamming the bottle down on the table, I growl, "You're a little overdressed for our lesson."

She licks her lips and then slowly pulls her sweater over her head, her tits swinging freely before me. Then she stares at me with hunger in her eyes as she shimmies out of her skirt, revealing nothing but a glistening pussy begging to be filled.

I remove my own clothes and stand naked before her, palming my cock and stroking it until it grows hard and ready.

She parts her thighs and I openly stare as her fingers dip between them, and she circles her clit, watching me the whole time. Then she whispers, "Do you like what you see?"

"I do." Dropping to my knees, I grab her ankles and pull her sharply toward me and bury my face between them, inhaling the scent of a woman who is begging for it and as I drag my tongue up her slick folds, I taste the sweet honey of a woman who knows what she wants.

As I suck her clit, she moans and grasps my hair, pulling me further in. "That feels so good." She purrs beneath me, and I feel my cock aching to fuck her hard, and as her legs wrap around my neck, she almost suffocates me.

Pulling back, I flick her around and land a swift blow to her ass for daring to take control, and she yelps with a mixture of pain and desire.

"Do you like it rough, Miss. English?"

She groans with longing and as I straddle her, I love seeing the redness of my mark flaring on her white, soft skin.

Reaching for my pants, I drag a condom from the

pocket and protect us both before plunging into her from behind in a swift move with no warning.

She cries out as I nail her to the bed and thrust inside with no regard, the headboard banging against the wall. Grabbing her hair, I fist it and pull down sharply and as she cries out, I fuck her hard and relentlessly.

She doesn't get the seduction or the gentle care that most women crave. She gets fucked like the whore she is because she demands it.

Her moans of pleasure make me drive harder, deeper and she cries out, "Fuck that feels so good." Pressing down on her back, I feel my shaft grazing her walls and then I pull out and turn her swiftly around and stare into her lust-filled eyes.

"On your knees, Miss. English."

Her heightened color tells me she was close and yet the excitement in her eyes tells me she wants this to last, so as I stand and she falls to her knees beside me, I thrust inside her willing mouth and face fuck her as I fist her hair and punish her without regard for her at all.

It feels amazing as she licks, sucks and grabs my balls firmly, squeezing them until I hiss, "That feels so good."

The fact this is so wrong makes it even more delicious and as I thrust inside her wet mouth, I feel like I'm in paradise.

Pulling out, I push her against the wall, knocking the lamp off the side and it crashes to the floor. "Fuck Angelo, you're out of control."

She giggles and I stare into her slightly crazed eyes and smirk. "You know it."

Then I wrap my shaft in another condom and growl, "Spread your legs."

Her breathing intensifies as I slam in hard and hold her wrists above her head, stretching her out before me like a sacrifice.

Lifting one leg over my arm, I drive in hard, just how she likes it, and bite down on her neck.

This is fucking at its most basic, and she is loving every second of it.

She comes so hard she screams like an animal and my own roar of release joins hers in the madness surrounding us.

She goes limp in my arms as her breath comes fast, panting as if she's running a race and as I pull out and toss the condom in the trash, she laughs softly. "I knew it would be good."

"Then you're as fucking twisted as I am if you like that shit." I laugh as she presses her body against mine and pulls me close, whispering, "I am every depraved dream you ever had, and nothing is too dirty. Let me show you how filthy sex can be. Let me teach you a lesson you'll thank me for, forever."

Now she's got my interest and I say huskily, "What do you have in mind?"

She whispers in my ear, "That would be telling. I want to blow your mind, Angelo. I've been wanting this for months. A night of uninterrupted pleasure with my big, bad boy. Let me show you how much better it is with a woman who knows how to please a man."

She bites down hard on my earlobe and my cock dances with delight. Then she fixes me with a hard look and her voice cuts like a whip through the air as she growls, "Lie on the bed. It's my turn now."

She pushes me back and hell, I've never been more

turned on in my life and as I lie down, the slight manic glint to her eye tells me this woman knows exactly what she wants and I'm about to have the night of my life.

I watch as she removes a blindfold from the drawer and purrs, "Trust me, baby, this is going to blow your mind."

Grinning, she grabs a bottle of beer from the cooler and with one hand slips the blindfold on me and then holds my head as she pushes the bottle between my lips. "Drink up baby. Feel the cool liquid filling you inside."

As I swallow the beer, she strokes my shaft gently and the feeling it creates is incredible. So many things are happening. The fact I can't see a thing, just feel. The effect of the beer inside me and the soft gentle way she holds me in her hands makes me long for more and as she dips her head, she whispers, "Drain that bottle while I drain you."

Fuck me, this is so intense and as I lean back against the pillows and swig the beer, she goes to work on my cock, sucking, tasting and licking it with her head between my legs. This feels like paradise and as lessons go, this one is shaping up to be the best one yet.

28

WINTER

Freedom is like a drug. I can almost taste it. It's surrounding me like an energy that I can feed from. Intoxicating, dangerous and destruction of the most devastating kind.

It's as if I'm having an out-of-body experience. The music, the lights, alcohol and laughter all merge into a delicious cocktail of delight, promising life changing consequences.

Here at the house next door, I am Winter Sontauro, ordinary girl, popular girl and foolish girl, all rolled into one and it never felt so good.

I've lost count of the drinks I've had when no one was looking. The number of guys I've danced with and moved on to the next before they can take anything further. I've danced with Claudia, Emma and several girls whose names I never registered, and, like Cinderella, I am experiencing the night of my life. However, also like Cinderella, when the clock strikes twelve, it all turns to dust and as I turn to move away from the guy who thinks he stands a chance with me, he pulls me back with a drunken, "Where do you think you're going?"

He pulls me close and goes in for a sloppy kiss and before I know what's happening a hard body forces itself between us and I hear the deep chilling tones of my rescuer, "Fuck off before I kill you."

I stare up in surprise at a wall of muscle and violence and see Ivan glaring at the terrified senior, who backs off immediately. "I'm sorry, man, I didn't..."

Ivan just pushes him away and grabs my arm, whispering, "Party's over, princess."

"No."

I feel so angry I can hardly speak, and he whispers, "Don't make a scene; you know how this works."

My situation comes back and hits me hard and the surrounding laughter of people living their best lives makes it an even more bitter pill to swallow when I realize this will never be my life.

With a sigh of resignation, I allow myself to be pulled from the room and as we step into the fresh air, I feel the tears stinging behind my eyes.

The moon beams down with a sympathetic smile and I raise my eyes to it and wish hard for a different life than the one I've been sentenced to.

Then I hear a soft, "I'm sorry, angel."

I look at the savage beside me and he smiles, which shocks me more than anything. Ivan doesn't wear humanity well, and I'm surprised to see the sadness in his eyes as he sighs and places his arm around my shaking shoulders.

"This life sucks for all of us, but you get the worst of it. I wish you had more freedom, Winter, but this is for your own good."

"Is it though, Ivan, because from where I'm standing, I'm struggling to see any good in my life?"

He pulls me closer and says bitterly, "Good is for the ordinary people. Guys who don't know how lucky they are. Girls who think they have it all, but when the sun breaks on the rest of their lives, will discover they're not so special after all. You're special, Winter. More than you realize because you have something they will never have, strength, bravery and a sense of duty."

I'm surprised to hear him actually speaking to me because he doesn't normally say much. He just grunts and looks angry most of the time and I wonder about him.

"What about you, Ivan? Do you fear the future because I'm guessing yours is not much better than mine?"

He shrugs. "I know no different and I expect nothing more. You see, that's where I'm luckier than the rest of us because I don't dream. I just accept the nightmares and make them part of my soul."

I feel sorry for him, and it must show on my face because he shakes his head. "Don't pity me. I made peace with this life years ago. When I leave Rockwell Academy, I'm not taking fear with me and if I sound like a bastard, it's because I am. What's happening to you is not acceptable but not uncommon in our lives. You've always known what will happen, just not the players involved. Just own your future and whatever happens, make it on your terms. Don't be a victim and be strong."

"Like you." He smiles and the moon lights up the gleam in eyes that hold the dark secrets of hell in them, and he says in a sharp voice, "I am strong because I won't allow myself to be anything less. Talking of which..." He sighs. "I have to go, which is why your night ends now."

"Where?"

I'm confused, and he says tightly, "Duty calls."

"Ivan." A familiar voice cuts through the darkness, making me shiver inside and as Alessandro steps into the light, Ivan sighs. "Sorry my friend, but I have to pass this over to you. Just make sure she gets home in one piece."

His voice has a ring of steel attached and Alessandro growls, "Fuck you, Ivan."

Harsh laughter surrounds me as he steps away and swaps places with a man who is possibly the most dangerous of them all—for my heart.

"Where's he going?" I'm curious as Alessandro takes his place and he shrugs. "He got a call from the guy who runs the fights in town. There's a heavy prize fund for whoever takes on an open ring and survives. This has his name written all over it and so he called me to take over watching you."

"Watching me, what the..."

Alessandro just shrugs. "Your brother's orders. Sorry baby, you know what he's like."

I feel so angry I can almost taste it and it must show on my face because Alessandro sighs. "Life's a bitch Winter, surely you know that by now and to be honest, I would do the same."

"Why?" I feel an edge to my voice that disappoints me because I thought he was different from the rest of them and he says gruffly, "Because you're better than those bitches in there. The thought of those jocks treating you like an ordinary girl, trying to take what they want with no regard for your feelings, makes me mad as hell."

My heart softens a little and I blink back the tears. "Maybe I want to be like them, Alessandro, just to see what all the fuss is about."

He turns and, in the moonlight, I see the danger in his eyes as he hisses, "I want better for you, Winter. I want you to have the world and I want to be the man to give it to you."

My breath hitches when I see the rage flashing in his eyes and he has never looked more desirable than now.

He shakes himself and smiles ruefully. "Come, we need to get back. You've had long enough and we're still struggling to find the person messing with us."

It's only a short distance to the house and I wish it was in another State entirely because just having some time alone with the man who is never far from my thoughts is a pleasure I never saw coming. I'd rather be here with him, anyway, than at the party with someone else.

"Can we stop and talk?"

The words make it out before I can check them, and he stops in surprise. 'That may not be the best idea you've ever had, baby."

Just hearing his soft endearment makes the knife twist deeper and I shrug. "Possibly, but talking can't hurt, surely."

I nod to the wall beside the house and say almost desperately, "Please, just five minutes. I don't feel so good anyway and should sit down."

I pretend something to get me what I want, and his look of concern makes me feel like a bitch as I sway a little and act as if I've had too much to drink. However, desperate times call for desperate measures and I love how his hand finds mine, and he says with concern, "Of course, just breathe deeply."

He sweetly removes his jacket and drops it to the ground and gently helps me down to sit on it and as he settles beside me, I long to put my head on his shoulder and feel his arm wrap around me. But he's keeping his distance, probably because he values his friendship with my brother more than anything else.

"I wish I could think of a way out of this madness." I sigh and he nods. "I've thought of everything."

"What did you come up with?"

"A kind of plan, but I'm not sure it will work."

"I'm willing to try anything."

He laughs bitterly. "You may not like this one." Now I'm more than curious because his voice sounds gentler, more wistful even, and I whisper, "Tell me."

He turns and his eyes are like two black pools, glittering with emotion and it makes my breath hitch and time stand still as he says in a husky whisper, "We arrange your marriage to me."

"You." A dart of hope pierces my heart, and he nods. "My grandfather wants me to join him in the family business."

"In Sicily?"

He nods, the bitterness shrouding his eyes in madness. "He would do anything for me to agree on something I've refused and even my own father ran away from."

"Why?"

I'm confused because Alessandro is as fucked as the rest of us, and I wonder what options he has.

"My father broke away because he hates the tradition that Sicily demands. The goldfish bowl my grandfather lives in and the madness that surrounds that. In America, he enjoys a different kind of terror. He plays by his own rules and makes them up as he goes along. Petty crime mainly, prostitution and gambling. My father loves to play a part in that and is the evillest bastard I know, but my grandfather is both evil and powerful with a danger that runs like blood in his veins."

"I envy you have a choice."

He nods. "My father has made it clear I only have two options. He is wrong."

I shift closer, feeling his warmth wrapping me in comfort as he says roughly, "I have three as it happens, possibly four, even five."

"Which are?"

"Work with my father and lose my mind or return to Sicily and lose my freedom. Then there's my preferred one of leaving all the shit behind and buying me some time."

"How will you do that?"

"I made a deal with my grandfather behind my father's back."

I feel worried and whisper, "What deal?"

His low laugh of bitterness tells me it's a deal made with the devil, and he growls, "I get to follow my dream on a promise to take up his position when he can no longer do it himself."

"What is your dream?"

He sounds animated as he says, "I want to make movies. It's always fascinated me and I'm working toward that with my studies."

I wasn't expecting that, and I feel glad he has something like that in his life.

"So, my grandfather agreed to help me make it happen and give me a few years of freedom, at least, supposing he lives that long."

Reaching out, I grasp his hand and he looks at me in shock, which makes me smile sadly. "Follow your dream, Alessandro, for as long as you have it and enjoy every minute of it."

He shakes his head. "That was before I met you."

"What do you mean?" I'm confused, and he stares at me with an intensity that draws me in, and I can't look away as he reaches up and touches my cheek, almost as if he's afraid I'll disappear and whispers, "I intend on making a new deal with my grandfather. Arrange marriage to you and I'll return after graduation."

His words are like a bolt of lightning striking my heart, and I pull back in horror. "No!"

He looks crushed as I say angrily, "I will not allow you to give up your dream for me. That's not good."

He pulls my face up to look at him and I see the emotion burning deep in his eyes as he says roughly, "I will do anything to save you, Winter and even if you hate the thought of marriage to me, I will keep you safe. I won't force you to do anything you don't want to, and I'll give you space to enjoy as normal a life as I can give you."

"No, Alessandro, I can't let you sacrifice your future for me. I would never forgive myself." I break away. "Anyway, you said there was another option. Tell me."

He shrugs. "You'll have to ask your brother about that one. Maybe it's the best one because if it works, we will all be free - to a degree, anyway."

I make to speak, and he says firmly, "It's not for me to say, but I will do anything to save you, Winter, because…"

"Because what?" I lean a little closer and as we sit in the shadows, it's as if we are on our own private planet where the impossible becomes reality and he whispers, his lips hovering against mine, "Because I feel down deep in my heart that you are mine."

As the tears sparkle in my eyes, my heart breaks in two because I think I felt it as soon as I met him. The connection is strong, and the message is clear. Alessandro is the man my heart desires but can never have. Because in standing a chance with him, I do it by stepping over his dreams and grinding them to dust and I will never let him make that choice.

29

WINTER

A million thoughts race through my head as Alessandro pulls me to my feet and we walk silently back to the house. My situation is weighing heavily on my mind, and I am torn between clinging onto the lifeline he has thrown me and rejecting it out of hand.

We head inside and the house feels empty in the dead of night, and I whisper, "Where is everyone?"

He shrugs. "Malik is probably in his room monitoring the world on CCTV and who knows where Flynn is?"

"Is he ok?"

Alessandro nods. "He's fine."

I follow him to the kitchen and watch as he grabs some mugs from the cupboard and nods toward the barstool. "I'll make you a coffee to warm you up."

"Thanks."

As I watch him, I feast my eyes on a man crafted from my own dreams. His biceps are huge and his muscles ripple under the tight t-shirt he wears, and the low-rise jeans reveal an ass I long to feel in my hands. His hair is tied back tonight, revealing those broad shoulders and the stubble grazing his chin, makes me squirm on my seat because unlike the guys at the house next door, Alessandro is a man not a boy and I have never wanted to know what a man feels like—what *he* feels like, so much in my life.

Trying to distract my thoughts, I say with interest, "Tell me about Flynn. Why does he feel so much and then walk away?"

He sighs. "Because he hates feeling anything but can't help himself. He is like the rest of us, desperate for love and everything it brings, but afraid of how weak that makes him."

He turns and hands me the coffee, and his eyes glitter with anger. "No connections, no emotion. That's the only way we can survive, but it's not that easy sometimes."

"So, Flynn does care for Emma."

"Probably." He drops down on the stool beside me and leans on the counter, making me itch to trace my fingers over his broad biceps.

"Flynn allows himself to feel more than the rest of us and then struggles to kill those feelings afterward. He takes off, sometimes for days, and deals with it in his own way. When he returns, he brings a little more madness with him, and that worries me."

I fall silent because I've seen the madness in his eyes and know it's a very bad thing because one day it will destroy him in a far more devastating way than allowing himself to love someone and I feel concerned for him.

Alessandro sighs and says with a resignation I share, "Well, I'm heading to the sack. You should do the same."

He stands and I follow him and as we head to the stairs, I feel the loneliness wrapping me in bitterness.

We head upstairs, one behind the other and as he makes to turn right at the top of the first staircase, he growls, "Goodnight, Winter, and I'm sorry."

"About what?"

"For not being good enough."

He makes to go, and I reach out and grab his arm and whisper angrily, "Don't you dare say you're not good enough, Alessandro, you are..." I drop my hand and sigh. "Well... anyway, just don't."

I turn and walk away because I don't want to open my heart to him and let him step inside because, like Flynn, I don't think I could cope with the pain when he leaves.

As I head to my own room, I feel lonely and bitterly disappointed that my evening ended this way. For once, I was free, and it felt so good. It seems that all I want is the freedom to develop feelings for the man I've just left behind.

As I change and sit on my bed, I think about Emma and how amazing it proved for her. She traded her virginity for confidence, and she has no regrets.

The loneliness is depressing me, so I jump from my bed and head off to find her. Maybe she will let me stay with her because I don't want to be alone, not tonight.

As I push my way into her room, the moonlight illuminates the empty bed and I sigh. She's not back, which tells me she's enjoying a much better night than me.

Picturing the happiness on her face when she told me

how amazing it was with Flynn and that she never regretted a thing, makes me long for that same experience.

Maybe it's the alcohol and maybe it's the effects of the past twenty-four hours, but Alessandro's words return to haunt me. Could I accept his offer and allow him to arrange our marriage? What would that feel like?

Then I think of his future and the chance of making his dreams come true and know I can never be the one to take that from him. Then I think of my future and the pain hits me hard. It's an impossible situation that I can see no way out of.

Looking at Emma's empty bed, I see my future flash before my eyes. A cold, emotionless future, with a man who will use my body to bear children and treat me like another employee. I know how it works. I've been told as much by my father. Just picturing his evil, twisted face, snarling at me, telling me my role is to spread my legs and do what my husband tells me. Never complain and never expect anything more than a good hard fuck and if I'm lucky, that's all I'll get. I'm to marry to give my father protection. A rival family that will merge with my own and make us stronger. That's all I am, a commodity, and it hurts like hell.

Then the madness really takes hold as an idea sparks in my mind. Can I really have my one night only? To gift myself the dream for a brief moment of time. To make my own decision about what I do with my body and if the consequences of that end my life on my marital bed, I will have had a lucky escape from a lifetime of madness.

My heart quickens as I sense change coming. Something that I can do for myself and fuck the consequences. I know just where I'm heading and if I'm rejected, then at least I tried.

Feeling a little giddy with excitement, I push the door to Emma's room open and walk silently down the hallway, my stomach churning.

As I creep down the stairs, a thousand reasons why I should head back the way I came argues with my impetuous foolishness. But I push them away because I want this more than I want my life to continue and so, as I retrace my footsteps and head to Alessandro's room, I feel my heart thumping out of control. This is madness, certifiable madness that will only end badly, but I can't deal with that right now. I am driven by lust and a sense of doing something for me, for once in my life. For one night only, what can be wrong about that?

I ALMOST BACK OUT as I pass silently through the hallway and head toward his room. What am I thinking? I will look desperate. A fool. Madness clothed in depravity because I want just one night with him.

A faint sound from another room makes my heart quicken. Malik's room. Will he come out and find me creeping through the darkness? If anything, it spurs me on faster and as I reach Alessandro's door, I think my heart can knock on it for me because it is banging so loudly, I can hear nothing else. My mouth is dry and there's a buzzing in my head, but the sense of anticipation is a delicious taste on my tongue because I have never felt so alive. I'm really doing this–something for myself because it's what *I* want. Taking charge of my life to give me a delicious memory to cherish and do something on my own terms, for once.

I have never felt surer of anything in my life before and I don't think of the consequences, just of what I want.

Is this madness or destiny? I'm about to find out, so I turn the handle and open the door a crack, the darkness in the room telling me its occupant has turned in for the night.

Slipping inside, I close the door quietly and feel my heart race as I edge through the darkness and whisper, "Alessandro."

There's nothing but a slight movement and it's not coming from the direction of the bed. My heart races as a low voice growls, "Go back to your room, Winter."

It makes me jump and I peer through the darkness and swallow hard as the moonlight picks out the man I've come to find and I say softly, "I came to ask you a favor."

"Denied, leave."

His voice is rough with an edge to it that should have me backing away, but I feel emboldened by alcohol and say firmly, "No. I want you to do something for me and if you won't, I'll find someone who will."

Like lightning striking its unfortunate victim, he crosses the room and grabs my hand, pulling me toward him sharply and crushing me against his body. His strong arms lock around my waist and he dips his head and growls, "Not fucking likely."

My heart beats so fast I can't keep up and I say with a hitch in my voice, "Please, Alessandro, one night only. It has to be you."

For a moment there's silence and all I hear is the sound of the clock ticking down to my eternal damnation and he says with a hint of sadness, "Don't you think I want this more than anything?" His words are so soft I strain to hear them, and he sighs. "I want you so much, I'm losing my mind. I can't sleep. I can't fucking operate because you are all I see. But I can't. It would seal your death warrant and how could I live with myself knowing I caused an angel to fall? Your brother would kill me, and I'd welcome the release from a lifetime of madness that would sentence me to."

He pulls me toward him so hard it knocks the air from my lungs, and he growls, "You are asking for the impossible."

Reaching up, I touch his face, loving how the stubble grazes sharply against my hand. I fix him with my most desperate look and say slightly broken, "Please, just one night, it must be you. Don't you think I know what I'm asking, the danger I'm putting us both in. I can't see past this need inside me to experience something so beautiful it can only come from you. Just thinking of my first time being with a man my father chooses makes my soul weep. I need this and I know I'm asking a lot, but if I have just one amazing memory, I can cope with the rest of the shit that follows."

Leaning against his chest, I love how he smells. Musky, the scent of a man, *my man* and I need to know what that feels like.

He pulls back a little and raises my face to his and I watch his dark eyes glittering with emotion as he growls, "I can refuse you nothing, Winter, but I know I must try. This is a bad decision that should never be allowed to happen."

"Please, Alessandro, I'm begging you to make this one time count. Please, if it's the last thing I ever do, I want it to be with you."

His lips crash against mine with a hunger that sends me

reeling. The desperate kiss of a lover in impossible circumstances. Hard, demanding and possessive, desperate even as his tongue clashes with mine as he holds my head in his hands.

He devours me, enters my personal space and sets up home. We kiss like star-crossed lovers in waiting because that's exactly how it feels. His growl of desperation matches the one inside me and as he pulls away, I feel as if he takes my will to survive along with him.

Panicking slightly, I say huskily, "It has to be you; no one will ever know. Please, this is the only thing I want."

A battle plays across his face, and I watch it, holding my breath. A thousand emotions flood the room in a very short space of time and then he says darkly, "On my terms only."

"Which are?"

"You marry me."

My heart dives because I know what that involves, and the determination in his eyes tells me it's an unconditional requirement.

Nodding, I take a deep breath and say, "Ok."

"You will?" He stares at me as if stepping into my soul and I nod, keeping emotion from playing any part in this. "I agree, Alessandro. Make the call and do what you must. Set me free and I'll always be yours."

The words stick in my throat because this is the last thing I want him to promise me, but I already know it's the only condition and the only way I'll get what I want—him.

His eyes sparkle with lust and I hitch my breath because now I've started something I'm not sure either of us will survive.

30

WINTER

Alessandro takes my hand and pulls me close with less urgency and more care and whispers, "Are you sure about this, baby?"

I swallow the lump in my throat and nod. "I am."

He traces a light trail down my face and stares at me in wonder and as he lowers his lips to mine, I taste a softer side of him. Tentatively, I reach up and run my fingers through his hair and my heart leaps as I anticipate what this leads to.

Then he pulls back and his eyes shine in the moonlight as he removes his t-shirt and my heart flutters at the muscles dancing before my eyes. The realization of what I've done is swirling around me like a bad smell. I want it to go away, to let me enjoy this moment, but it just taunts me and reminds me what an idiot I am. Can he protect me; will he ride in and save me? Regardless of that, I want my one night with him, anyway.

So, I lift my own top off and love how his eyes brim with lust-filled energy and as I reach for my pants, he does the same and we remove them in sync, both staring into the abyss together. The edge of the abyss is the name of this house, and it certainly lives up to its name in this moment.

Standing naked in the darkness with just the light of the moon is an erotic experience that I have only dreamed of before.

I stare at his huge cock that stands proudly erect and shiver as I imagine what that will do to me and he whispers, "Last chance to back out, Winter. Step away from this madness and we will never speak of it again."

"No." My voice is hoarse, and I move toward his bed, lowering myself to sit on the edge and then shimmy back against the pillows. "I need this. I need you."

My voice is firm, and I know I would break apart if he refused me something I need more than my life it seems and with a low growl, he advances, sitting beside me on the bed and running his hand up my leg.

I shiver with anticipation as he lowers his lips and kisses a trail from my feet to my drenched pussy and then I gasp as he pushes my legs apart and runs his tongue along the length of me before capturing my clit and sucking it gently. I moan softly and he lifts his head and whispers, "No noise. Do you think you can be silent, baby?"

I nod, feeling so out of my depth, and as he licks and sucks the part of me no one has ever seen before, I start to see what the fuss is all about.

I never knew I could feel this way. Physically ache for something I don't know the first thing about. Just feeling him worshipping my body is such a powerful emotion and I want to weep tears of pleasure because, finally, I'm getting something I've thought of so many times under my own hand at night beneath the covers. That is nothing like this though and as he continues exploring my body, licking, biting and marking me, I take great pleasure in every single touch. It's as if he's playing my body like a musician and it feels amazing.

My nipples harden against his tongue and his low growl of pleasure makes me feel proud that I can do this. He must have been with hundreds of girls before, and I wonder if he is this tender with them. He reaches my mouth and I taste my own arousal on his tongue, which only makes me more frantic to feel him inside me, owning me, claiming me and ridding me of something that will be my ultimate downfall because if I make it to my wedding night with someone else, I may as well kill myself before he gets that pleasure.

Just feeling his hard length against me turns me on and I gasp as he rubs his shaft against me. I am throbbing and need to feel him inside and as his fingers pinch and push against my clit, I feel the longing burst through me as delirium takes over.

Nothing else matters but this. Alessandro and this moment. He whispers in my ear, "Wait one second."

I hear him fumbling for a condom and as he tears the wrapper, I say with a groan, "No."

"Yes."

"I'm on the pill. It's fine."

"You're what! Since when?"

He pulls back and looks quite angry about that, and I smile. "Since puberty, actually. For my periods. Cramps are a bitch."

"Even so. It's for your own protection."

"Please." Reaching down, I close my hand over his and whisper, "One night only. I want the whole of you. Nothing between us and everything you've got."

I know he's battling with this, but I don't care and leaning in, I capture his lips and kiss him so hard he drops the condom on the wooden floor below and the passion in him lights a fuse that is now burning out of control and can't be stopped.

He says in a soft voice, "This will hurt, but not for long."

I nod because now the moment is here, I can't quite believe it's happening, and I prepare myself for a one time experience I will revisit many times in the future in my mind.

He stares into my eyes the entire time as he eases in slowly and gently. He forces past the resistance as my body wakes up and realizes something different is happening. The sharp pain causes my breath to hitch, and his mouth fastens over mine as I cry out, muffling the sound and keeping the wolf from the door.

It hurts so much; as if he's set fire to me inside and yet as the burn fades, all that's left is a sense of fulfillment. Feeling him inside me is a powerful thing and as he looks into my eyes, I stare right back with a smile of pleasure only he can give me. He moves gently, slowly and with care and if I feel anything at this moment, it's an intense love for this man. He drags his thumb against my clit, applying delicious pressure and as my body relaxes around his hard cock, it sighs and settles into its new home.

My breasts graze against his chest and his body is flush with mine and we fit together perfectly. There is no hurry to finish this anytime soon and as we move together in perfect time, I feel a burst of emotion that makes this the best experience of my life. I'm making love to Alessandro Majerio and if my life ends tomorrow, I will consider I lived my best life, anyway.

Girl becomes woman, and it is every bit as wonderful as I imagined and as the strangest feeling builds inside me, I take a peek into heaven as the light explodes through my body and the sweetest feeling in the world carries me on a wave of pleasure right back down to earth.

31

ANGELO

The first thing I'm aware of is that I'm not in my own bed. As my eyes open, I see the pink walls and feel as if I ache all over. My mind struggles to wake up and as I look around me, I take in the unfamiliar surroundings and then the memory returns.

Fuck me, what a night.

I look to the side and see the empty space beside me and try to drag myself up but feel as if my limbs are made of clouds.

I feel so weak, and my body burns as if a thousand cigarettes have been extinguished on my dick.

I notice the time on the clock on the wall and groan. 10 am, what the fuck?

The sun is high outside, telling me I've been here for over twelve hours and then I hear a soft giggle as the door opens and Miss. English heads into the room dressed for class.

"Hey, sleepyhead, you made it back."

"What happened?" I groan as I try to make my limbs

work and she sits beside me on the bed and pushes the hair from my eyes. "We made a night of it and honey; you were a legend."

"Then why do I feel like shit?" My throat is dry and my breathing uneven, and then it hits me. This isn't normal. Did she drug me or something?

Thinking back on the bottles of beer she fed me on repeat, I wonder if they contained more than alcohol. Quickly, I reach out and grab her wrist and snarl. "What do you give me?"

She snatches it back from my weakened grasp and giggles. "The night of your life, honey. That's all it was and putting it simply, I fucked your brains out. Now, all good things must come to an end, and we need to get you out of here without anyone seeing you leave."

She grabs my clothes and thrusts them toward me and says firmly, "I'll head off and you can leave the way you came. Make sure it's when class has started and keep to the treeline. The last thing we need is word getting out about this."

She stands and then, as an afterthought, sits back down and presses her lips to mine. She tastes of toothpaste and cherry lip gloss and when she pulls back, whispers, "Just for the record, you were an amazing fuck. Then again, I always knew you would be."

She winks and leaves, slamming the door on her way out.

I dress quickly and think about what happened. Fuck, what was I thinking? I lost control for once in my life and I hate how that makes me feel.

A thousand thoughts spin through my mind, but I can't remember a fucking thing about last night past the moment where she placed the blindfold over my eyes and sucked me off while I drank beer.

I always knew she was a wild one but quite honestly, I can live without shit like that because what's the point if you can't remember and if anything, I feel violated, dirty even and wish I never came.

Sighing, I make my way outside and drag in deep lungful's of much-needed air.

I need to clear my head and get back to business because there is something making me uneasy about life at Rockwell ever since Winter came to stay.

I MAKE it back and the house is empty when I stumble inside, still a little unsteady on my legs. I head straight to the kitchen and fix myself a coffee and some toast because I need to get some food and drink inside me to help counteract how sick I feel.

"You look like shit."

I look around and see Flynn heading downstairs and I take in the huge black circles under his eyes and note his grazed knuckles. "I could say the same about you."

He heads into the kitchen and nods at the coffee. "Is there one of those for me?"

Pushing mine toward him, I pour another, and he groans. "Fuck, what a night."

"What happened?"

"Usual shit."

"Then tell me."

He sighs heavily. "I went to town and ended up in a bar and had too many to drink and picked a fight with a guy hitting on a girl. I ended up rearranging his face into a more interesting one and escorted the girl home. She invited me in and turned out to be a more grateful than I realized. We spent the night fucking Emma out of my head and now I'm good."

"What about Emma? Will it be ok living under the same roof?"

He yawns. "Sure, she's good about it. Knows it was one night of pleasure and has moved on already."

"She has?" I'm surprised, thinking of the frightened friend of my sister, and he grins, a little sadness dancing in his eyes. "I followed her to the party with Winter and watched them. Some guy latched on to Emma and they ended up making out in the shadows outside the house."

"You watched! What are you, some kind of pervert now?"

I laugh as he grins. "Never pretended otherwise. No, I was just checking she was ok with it."

"And was she?"

"Seemed that way. I heard them arrange to meet for breakfast and all that soppy shit couples speak to one another when they part company."

He sighs heavily. "My job is done. One frightened girl made into a woman overnight and able to take on the world. It's a public service. What can I say? I'm her guardian angel."

He grins. "Tell me what happened to you. I'm enjoying seeing this new side of you."

"What the fuck are you talking about?"

"The untidy hair, the stubble on your face and the shadows under your eyes. That you're still in yesterday's clothes and the fact you stink like you've attended a whore house and fucked every one of them multiple times."

"Miss. English."

Laughing loudly, he thumps his fist on the counter and howls like a wolf.

"Then sign me up for history, you lucky bastard."

"Yeah, well, enough about that. Do you know if Winter was ok at the party?"

"I think so. I saw Ivan at breakfast, and he said she left around twelve. He looked fucked though, man."

"How?" I feel irritated thinking of him hitting on the girls at the party rather than do his job of looking out for my sister.

Flynn grins. "Apparently, once your sister was safely escorted from the party, he headed into town for an open fight. Turns out he went up against at least eight men and it was only stopped when someone called the cops. The rest hightailed it out of there and he looks as if someone used his head to batter a door down."

"Did he win?"

"What do you think? Three thousand dollars richer and wearing a smug bastard look on his face."

I nod and say in a low voice, "Did Malik find out the identity of the mask wearing bastard?"

"He didn't say. Just growled something about making a few calls and headed off to class. He'll report back to you before he tells us anything, anyway."

I hope to God he's found the information I need because that feeling of unease just won't go away.

Sighing, I mention the one man I should be most worried about and say bluntly, "Alessandro?"

Flynn shrugs. "By all accounts, he was in bed around one this morning and is sleeping in. Lazy bastard."

"And Winter?"

"Her schedule says she's got a study period, so she's probably sleeping in. I know I would. Mind you, she was moaning about an assignment that's due in, so is probably holed up with Emma somewhere doing what the rest of us manage to avoid most of the time—learning."

He yawns. "I'm off to bed. I need to sleep off the night I had, and I suggest you do the same."

He heads off and I think about my friends, my sister and the problem I can feel building. It's all around me, like a pandemic waiting to strike. There's something going on that's out of my control and while everything seems in place, I can't shake the feeling that a storm's about to hit that we may not survive.

32

WINTER

I hear voices and as I wake from a very deep sleep, I feel a hard object wrapped around my leg and strong arms holding me tight.

My eyes adjust to the surroundings, and it all comes flooding back. Alessandro.

For a moment, I think of what happened last night and feel the evidence of that between my legs. I did it. *We* did it and now we're going to burn in hell.

Shifting slightly, I love the low groan from the man beside me as he comes back to me and then we hear Flynn's laughter from somewhere nearby and we both tense at the same time.

Fuck, its morning, and we fell asleep. This is bad.

I turn to face him and love how that makes me feel. It's so good to wake up in his arms and just thinking it's the only time makes me sad. If I see any regret in his eyes, it's well hidden and just the emotion in them tells me he's feeling the same.

Once again, we hear laughter and the howl of a wolf

and Alessandro places his finger against my lips and whispers, "This is bad."

I nod as we lie stiff, almost in shock, and then he moves slowly and carefully and reaches for his clothes.

I watch him dress and admire his naked perfection as he covers a body I would die to look at for the rest of my life and then he leans down and kisses me long, leisurely and so sweetly, I feel my body coming alive ready to welcome him in once more.

"Thank you." He whispers against my lips and then says in the softest voice, "I'll distract them while you head upstairs. Pretend you're hung over or something."

I nod and he winks as he heads toward the door and I say softly, "Thank you and just so you know, I don't regret a thing."

He nods and blows me a kiss and then he's gone before I can say anything to embarrass myself, like declare my undying love for him, or something along those lines. But I do. I know I do and yet how can that ever develop into something amazing? It was just a fleeting moment in a lifetime of bitter regret. One moment of pleasure that will have to stay with me forever and keep my heart wrapped in a bubble of love.

I ache so badly as I reach for my clothes and as I quickly dress, I'm desperate for a long shower and something to eat.

Cracking open the door, I hear nothing and quietly tiptoe along the corridor and take the stairs to my room.

It's only when I'm safely inside that I relax and yet I can't keep the smile from my face as I revisit what happened last night.

I did it. I made something so beautiful, so magical,

happen and it was on my terms. I think I can deal with anything right now because we got away with it. Nobody found us and we enjoyed a night of pure unadulterated pleasure and now nothing can ever take that away from me.

IT'S ONLY when I hear the shower from Angelo's room, do I creep downstairs and head to class. I'm not sure how I'll disguise my feelings toward Alessandro, but I know I must, for his sake, more than mine. Nobody must know what happened last night—ever and as I slip into my seat in class, I congratulate myself on a plan coming together.

LATER, I meet Emma for lunch in the canteen and she looks at me with a smug expression. "Thanks for inviting me to that party, Winter. I had the best time."

She looks so happy I feel my heart sag with relief, and she leans closer and giggles. "You know, after Flynn I thought it wouldn't happen again. Not at Rockwell, anyway."

"What?" I feel confused, and she smiles dreamily. "Corey."

"The guy you were with. What happened?"

"Well..." She leans forward and looks around, checking no one's listening. "We went outside, and it was unbelievably romantic. The moon, the stars, the music from the house. It was peaceful out there and he was so attentive. He told me he'd always liked me and thought I wasn't interested. When he saw me at the party, he couldn't believe how amazing I looked and was glad he found the courage to talk to me."

"That's nice." I'm pleased for her, and she sighs.

"We made out under the stars, and it was so good. It felt natural, you know, like God was giving me his blessing to enjoy college life like the rest of them."

"You *are* like the rest of them."

I fix her with a look that pushes away any doubts of that and she says sadly, "I never felt like it. I was always the fat girl from maths, english, or science. The girl with more spots than a kid with chicken pox and who looks as if her mom still dresses her. I was bullied, ignored, and dismissed. But that all changed when I became your friend and you opened up a whole new world to me, so thank you, Winter. I owe you everything."

"And Flynn."

I grin as she blushes. "Yes, I owe Flynn a huge debt because he turned me into a woman, and I will never forget that."

Knowing exactly what she means, I say with curiosity, "Do you ever wish you could be with Flynn?"

A hint of sadness reaches her eyes, and she nods. "Of course. He is probably the best-looking guy I have ever seen with the most generous heart. He is seriously gorgeous inside and out and has this lost look about him that makes me feel like a protective mama bear. I adore that man and wish he was *my* man, but he made it clear that was never an option and I went into it knowing that. So, I accept his generous gift and use it wisely."

She laughs and I shake my head. "Corey."

She nods and sighs heavily. "We only made out last

night, but he wanted more. I even let him finger me. Can you believe I did that?"

"No, I can't."

Laughing, she leans forward and whispers, "I even returned the favor and he came in my hand. I'm guessing it won't be long before we end up going all the way and you know what? I can't wait."

Leaning back, she fixes me with a sympathetic look. "I'm sorry, Winter."

"What for?"

"I'm rattling on about something you can never have, not at Rockwell Academy all the time your brother has placed an imaginary chastity belt around you. It must suck being you sometimes."

"I'll live." I smile and think about Alessandro and wonder if we'll ever catch a break. Will his plan work, or will it just be a pipedream? More than anything, I want him to be my husband, but I'm not sure I like the idea of him giving up his own dream to make that happen.

33

ANGELO

I meet up with Malik after class and we head back to the house to discover his findings. He doesn't say much, but I see the steely glint in his eye that tells me he's discovered something at least and as soon as we're inside, we head to the kitchen as usual and grab some Gatorade.

"What you got?"

He wipes his mouth and throws me a hard stare. "Eden."

"What about her?"

"She's your masked intruder."

"That figures." For some reason, I feel better about that and laugh softly. "Revenge is sweet. Well, she certainly caused a ripple. I've got to hand it to her. How do you know?"

"I asked around and one of the girls told me her friend Brianna was bragging about it in the girl's locker room. Apparently, they wanted everyone to know they got back at you and made out it was a prank to get them back on top."

"Not much of a prank, sad really."

"Possibly, but what are you going to do about it?"

"Nothing. It's not worth the energy."

Knowing it was Eden, makes it ok somehow. I know she's just a vindictive bitch and I'm happy to let this one slide. Acknowledging it gives it an importance it doesn't deserve, so I yawn and laugh softly, "Well, that's a relief."

Malik nods. "How was your night?"

"Eventful." He raises his eyes as I fill him in and laughs. "Miss. English is a dark horse; I almost respect her. Then again..."

"What?"

He fixes me with a dark look. "Something feels off about it."

"You think?" I roll my eyes. "That woman is seriously fucked in the head. You should see her room, it's Barbie's Malibu mansion. She's a good fuck though. I'll give her credit for that."

Malik looks deep in thought, and I know what that usually means and say quickly, "What are you thinking?"

"That I need to run a few checks on our sexy, Miss. English. Something doesn't feel right."

He voices the thoughts in my own head, and I nod. "Agreed. I'm not sure why, but I lost part of last night."

"What do you mean?"

I've got his interest and I sigh. "I think she drugged me. It certainly felt like that."

Malik's eyes gleam with interest and I'm not surprised because he loves that kind of twisted fuckery himself. "What do you remember?"

"Just downing a beer blindfolded while she sucked my

dick. Then I woke up and felt as if I'd fought a war single-handed."

He looks thoughtful. "Leave it with me. I'll do a little digging."

Alessandro walks through the door and nods. "Man, I need a beer. Townsend was brutal today."

Thinking about our Phys Ed coach, I must agree with him. He's a bastard who loves pushing his students to breaking point and Alessandro looks wrecked. "I've crawled back here to recover. It doesn't help that Ivan wants to practice tonight, which is the last thing I feel like fucking doing."

He exhales sharply, and Malik grins. "You looked fucked, brother."

Alessandro looks up and I don't miss the look that passes between them, which sets me on edge. I'm not one to miss signs that something isn't right, and then Malik shrugs. "Anyway, I have a job to do. Catch you later."

He heads outside and I jerk my head toward him. "What was that all about?"

I stare at Alessandro hard, and he shrugs. "Fuck if I know. I gave up trying to work him out years ago."

He turns and heads out of the room, saying over his shoulder, "I'm off for a shower."

As I watch him go, something is making me uneasy. There are so many dangerous personalities in this house and I'm still trying to work them out. We may all be brothers here at Rockwell, but in the wider world we'll be enemies. Do I trust them? Not entirely, but they're the only hope I've got and if I'm to survive my future, they are the ones I'm counting on to have my back.

Later that afternoon, I'm heading out of class, and I see Eden and Brianna in the distance, whispering and smirking in my direction. Feeling pissed, I head their way and stop just short of them. Eden has that look of longing in her eyes that she's always directed at me, and I nod respectfully. "Eden."

"Angelo." She pulls herself up and thrusts out her chest and I note her freshly bleached hair that she's had styled into a bob cut, making her look way better than before. "We did you a favor. I like the hair." She blushes at my compliment and her eyes sparkle with longing. Brianna is looking at me as if I'm Santa fucking Claus and I laugh to myself because these girls are so transparent, it's funny. Despite what I did to them, they would still willingly spread their legs and after my lack of control last night, I'm feeling particularly devilish today.

"Fancy coming over later, both of you."

I stare at them with a lust-filled look and the look on their faces makes me almost laugh out loud. "Sure." They share a look and I know they would do anything asked and they are probably thinking this has brought them back in my favor. They always thought I admired a bitch at work and tried to work harder than most and so I lean forward and say huskily, "How do you fancy a threesome?"

Their wide eyes tell me this is a step they have never taken before and they look a little unsure, so I shrug. "Your loss." I turn away and Eden reaches out and grabs my arm, saying nervously, "What time?"

I turn slowly, "I know a place during history. Meet me at Miss. English's house."

"You're not serious." They look shocked and I grin like the devil I am.

"Wait for me in her bed, both of you naked and if you get cold, maybe you can start without me."

They share an anxious look and I whisper, "It's turning me on just thinking about it. You up for something different? I may even make it regular if I like it."

The promise that seals the deal because I know they would do anything to be considered one of us and so, as Eden licks her lips, she says huskily, "I'll be there."

Turning to Brianna, I see the flush to her cheeks as she nods. "Me too."

"Then I'll look forward to it. Ladies."

As I head off, I laugh to myself. Fuck, that was easy. This is going to be fun. As I round the corner, I take out my phone and punch in the text that will seal their final humiliation. Sometimes it's good to be me and for the first time in ages, I feel a lightness to my spirit that hasn't been there for some time.

34

WINTER

I am dreading going home later. Just having to sit with Alessandro at the dinner table is giving me palpitations. I want him so much. How can I keep that from my brother? One look and he will know something's up.

I can feel my situation weighing me down because what have I done? I'm no longer a virgin. I've sacrificed the only thing that's keeping me alive — my virginity.

My heart starts racing as I think about what that could mean—for me. Picturing my wedding night when my husband expects to see the evidence staining his sheets fills me with horror. I need to think this through because I'm guessing he wouldn't think twice about taking a knife to my throat and draining the blood from me another way when he learns his collateral is damaged.

I feel so afraid because even though Alessandro assured me his grandfather would make it happen, I still don't feel good about destroying his own dream of making movies. What have I done? I'm so selfish.

I don't think I hear a word Miss. English says and as the bell rings, she says firmly, "Winter–a word."

As the class files out, I remain behind, and she calls me forward to stand by her desk.

"Is everything ok?"

She looks concerned and just seeing her pretty smile and sparkling blue eyes remind me how starved I am of a female to look up to.

My lip trembles and she gasps, "Honey, what is it? You're shaking. What happened?"

"It's nothing, really."

I glance around me nervously and she says with a sigh. "Come on. I know exactly what you need."

She grabs her purse from her desk drawer and smiles. "A change of scene."

I follow her, feeling a little confused and as we head outside, she points to the staff parking lot.

"We can head into town and grab a soda, my treat, and then you can tell me what's bothering you."

Her smart red sports car is gleaming in the sunlight and to be honest, I could use a change of scene, so I step inside gratefully and buckle up and am glad to see the back of Rockwell Academy for a few hours at least.

Just speeding through the countryside reminds me of normal life and I love seeing the trees and wildflowers dancing in the breeze. It's as if the open-topped car is bathing my soul in balm as I let go of my problems and switch my mind off for a while.

Miss. English turns on the radio and the sweet country tunes of love and a simple life make me relax and after a while she says with a giggle. "This is fun, isn't it? You know, Rockwell Academy can be hard to take sometimes."

I nod. "You've got that right."

She grins mischievously. "You know, honey, I'm not much older than you are and like to cut loose from time to time. I'm guessing you don't have that same pleasure and I wonder if you fancy doing something a bit wild."

"Like what?"

She shrugs. "I don't know. Head to a bar, go dancing, get hit on by a couple of guys. We don't have to be back until later; what do you say?"

It sounds so tempting and I feel myself relax knowing I'm safe with her and I smile. "Sure, it sounds like fun."

We head toward the town and just before we hit the border, she says loudly, "I'm so stupid, sorry, do you mind?"

"What?"

"I promised I'd deliver a parcel to someone, and it's not far. Is that ok with you? It won't take a minute, and then we can head into town."

"Sure, no problem."

To be honest, I don't think anything of it because I wouldn't care if she drove across State. I'm just enjoying my freedom away from the mess I've made, and she sighs with relief. "Thanks, honey, I'll make it up to you."

We listen to the radio and before long head past the trees to a track off the road. As we bump along it, I look ahead and see some huge steel gates opening as we approach.

"What is this place?"

I'm curious because it looks expensive, and she laughs. "A friend of mine owns it. Impressive, isn't it?"

I look at the tree-lined driveway and see a huge mansion house in the distance all white and gleaming, looking like new.

"It's amazing. How do you know them?" I'm curious about where we're going, and she says lightly.

"We met a few years back when I was in college. Not far from here, actually, and I work for them on the odd occasion. It's all good and pays to have rich friends."

She pats the steering wheel. "Take this sweet baby. Not afforded on a teacher's pay, that's for sure. I do the odd favor for my friend, and he pays me well above the minimum wage limit."

"What do you do?"

I wonder if she does private tutoring. It would certainly make sense, and she smiles. "Oh, this and that, nothing too taxing."

We stop outside and she smiles. "Come and meet him; you'll get along really well."

I'm not sure if that's such a good idea. I've always been told to never trust strangers and if my father could see me now, he would be mad with rage. Maybe that's why I just smile and reach for the door handle. "Great, if you're sure he won't mind."

We head toward the huge wooden door, and she rings the bell, then we hear footsteps approaching. The door swings open, and a uniformed maid looks at us with interest.

"We're here to see the boss." Miss. English smiles and the woman nods and says politely, "Of course. Please come in."

As we step inside, I look around with interest and take in the expensive interior of a house that has everything in its place. It's pleasant enough; a little too ornate for my own tastes, but as we follow the woman into a large light-filled room, I wonder what this man does to earn a living.

The door closes behind us and Miss. English looks at her watch. "This shouldn't take long."

It suddenly strikes me that she's forgotten to bring the parcel in, and I whisper, "You've forgotten the parcel."

She rolls her eyes and laughs out loud. "I'm so stupid. Wait there, I'll go and fetch it."

As she heads out, I feel a little uncomfortable because now I'm alone, it feels wrong being here.

The time passes and after about ten minutes, I start feeling nervous. Where is she?

Another ten minutes pass and I decide to go and look for her but when I try the door, it won't budge.

I shake it and hope it's just stuck, but there's no moving it and then I hear a low husky voice say from across the room, "Hello, Winter."

Spinning around, I see a man who looks as old as my father and just as sinister. My heart sinks as I sense I've walked into something I'm not going to like and I say nervously, "I'm sorry, Miss. English is…"

"Gone."

He nods toward a chair and says smoothly, "Sit."

My legs shake as I do as he says and as he crosses the room, he steps into the light, and I take a look at a man who drives blades against my nerves and causes me to break out in a sweat. I know this man. Massimo Delauren, a friend of my father's and his reputation is not a good one. Rich, powerful and fucked-up and he is looking at me as if I'm his next meal.

"You have grown into a beautiful woman. I am pleased."

"What do you want?" I'm guessing I know already, and he laughs. "I want you, Winter. I always have, and your father has made a deal to deliver you to me."

"He never told me about this deal. I want to see him."

I sound brave, but inside I'm shaking, and he grins, revealing a perfect set of veneers. Despite his smart clothes and designer smile, he is still the ugliest man I have ever seen. His gray hair that's thinning on top and his slight paunch revolt me to the point I feel like hurling on his pure white carpet.

"Let me tell you a story, my dear. From the moment you were born, your father promised you to me. A wife in waiting and the most valuable asset he owns. As soon as you graduated, you would be mine. The prize in my collection and my finest treasure."

His eyes flash as he devours me with one sadistic look and says, "My wife, who I will adore. Show the world how lucky I am to have the best. My little pet, who I will look after and keep safe, and in return I granted your father my support in his business. An ally of the most influential kind who will keep his enemies away. A brilliant plan that satisfies all involved and now I have run out of patience.

I squirm on my seat and look for a chance to run because fuck this, I'm getting out of here and losing myself for good. Anything but this and as he reaches out and strokes my head like a pet dog, he exhales and closes his eyes as if enjoying a personal moment.

"I won't do it." I shatter his perfect moment, but he just laughs again. "I thought you'd say that. In fact, I hoped you would, so come with me and let me show you why you really have no choice in the matter."

Nervously, I stand and ignoring his outstretched hand, I walk beside him to the door he came through that leads into a corridor that's way darker than the rest of the rooms.

It feels cold and oppressive, and I shiver as he laughs like a twisted demon.

"Come, I have something extremely delicious to show you."

We head down some stone steps set into the wall and the air turns cooler and darker and I falter a little. "I'm not…"

Reaching out, he grabs my hand and growls, "You have no choice."

We reach the bottom step, and he pulls me roughly along with him, and I already know I'm powerless against him. He's too strong, so I must keep my cool and work out an escape plan.

He reaches what appears to be a cell door and his fingerprint opens it and when he switches on the light, I feel my heart thumping wildly and swallow the bile rising in my throat because I know that guy and it's not looking good.

"Here's my latest toy, Winter. I believe you may recognize him."

I can't look and Massimo says roughly, "Look at him."

He twists my head, forcing me to look at Emma's new boyfriend, Corey, stripped naked and chained to the wall. He looks terrified and blue from cold and his large, frightened eyes stare at me with hope that I can help him in some way.

Massimo slams the door behind us and heads toward him and I feel sick as he runs his hands down his body and gently strokes his cock. Corey looks as if he's going to be sick and Massimo purrs, "My beautiful boy; a very welcome addition to my collection."

"Your collection?" My voice sounds as weak as I feel

inside, and he nods. "Yes, I have several toys like this one that I play with from time to time. Mainly in my homes around the country, a few here, a few there. This is the third one I've had from Miss. English. She's such a good friend."

"Miss. English!" I feel sick as he nods. "Yes, the perfect agent for my needs. She delivers me fresh toys and I pay her well. A mutually beneficial arrangement and one I'm keen to continue."

He smiles with the twisted look of a predator and sighs as he presses his lips to Corey's who struggles as Massimo groans with longing. Then he stands and heads toward me and I back against the door, hoping I can get the hell out of here. "You see, my darling wife, I'm not interested in you sexually. I prefer boys. But I need a figurehead. Someone who plays the part and looks the part. Someone I can play with in another way. A perfect doll for me to dress and style their hair. My little china doll, who I will always treasure."

"I said no! You disgust me, so you may as well kill me now, you sick bastard."

He strikes me hard across the face and as my head snaps back, it hits the wall behind me, making me dizzy and he says almost apologetically, "Now you've made me spoil the goods. Naughty girls need to be punished, and you will soon learn that you have no choice."

He grabs me roughly and pulls me from the room, leaving Corey tied to the wall, shaking in fright. He opens the door of a cell next door and I blink when I see a very different set up. This one is painted white and padded everywhere. There's a huge white cage set in the center, decorated with roses, with a small swing hanging from the roof bars. In one swift move, he pushes me inside and locks the door, saying happily, "Welcome to your new cage, little bird. Say hi to your new home until you agree to my terms."

"And if I don't?" I try to get my breathing under control, and he laughs almost with pleasure.

"Then the next boy you see chained to the wall next door will be your brother. Once I have used him for my own pleasure and then cut him into pieces, he will be replaced by each of his friends. Their fate is in your hands, my dear wife. Become my perfect doll and they will be spared. Resist me and they will end up like your young friend next door."

He turns to leave, and I say quickly, "If I agree, will you set Corey free?"

He almost looks amused. "But where's the fun in that, my darling? No, you may listen to his screams to remind you what happens when you think you have a choice. Now, if you'll excuse me, I have business to attend to. Enjoy your stay and if you agree to be my wife, then you will be treated like a queen and spared from witnessing my hobby firsthand."

He turns and the door slams behind him and I feel my legs shake with fear. How has this happened? What the fuck has my father agreed to and, more importantly, what the hell am I going to do about this?

The screams from the next cell tear my heart in two. The sound of it is like a knife slashing me a thousand times. The begging and the cries of pain ring through my ears as I imagine the worst for Emma's guy. It must go on for hours and then it goes silent and the only sound I hear are my own sobs of terror. Just imagining any one of the guys dragged here and suffering the same fate makes my decision for me and then Baron's words come back to me when I need them most.

'Be smart, take it all in, learn how to survive and always look for their weakness because there always is one. Then use that to your advantage to get what you want.'

I will bide my time and work out my plan and when he is at his weakest point, I will kill Massimo Delauren and make it slow, painful and final.

35

ANGELO

I feel almost joyful as I head toward Miss. English's house with Alessandro walking beside me, and Ivan and Flynn behind us. Malik is waiting back at the house to monitor events on his cameras and as we walk, it feels good to be doing something like this. It's been a while and I'm looking forward to proving that nobody gets one over on us.

We push the door open, and Ivan and Flynn cover the exit as Alessandro preps his phone and I call out, "Have you done as I asked?"

A timid voice calls out, "Yes." She sounds nervous, completely unlike her usual sassy self, and I share a grin with my friend and say loudly, "I want you to touch each other. Pretend you're with a man and do what comes naturally. When I walk through that door, I want to see Eden's face between Brianna's legs, licking her wet pussy."

I give them a moment and then place my hand on the door and push it slightly open. I see the blonde bob between Brianna's legs and laugh to myself. They are both naked and appear to be doing everything I asked, and I say huskily, "I'm going to enter Eden from behind, poke your ass in the air and carry on what you're doing, if I don't hear Brianna come, you don't get to."

Alessandro holds up the phone and as I fling open the door, he videos the whole scene and as Brianna opens her eyes, she screams when she sees our amused faces as we film her worst nightmare and Eden pulls back and yells, "What the fuck?"

"Payback, bitches. A photograph for a moving one. Enjoy your moment of fame. I know I will."

We take a moment to appreciate the anger and humiliation in their eyes and as we leave, we hear, "You fucking bastards, give me that phone."

As Eden rushes out of the room stark naked, Ivan stands in her way and Flynn laughs as if he's just seen the funniest thing ever.

Eden turns whiter than her hair and slams the door in our faces and we leave them to work out their next move and head home. Alessandro sends the video to Malik who will distribute it to every phone on campus, and I wonder if Eden and Brianna will ever recover from this one.

Later that evening, we're no longer smiling.

Winter hasn't come home and I'm getting anxious. Emma came home hours ago looking pissed at something and Flynn said casually, "What's up, Angel?"

"Nothing, it's fine."

She makes to move past him, and he rests his hand on her arm and says softly, "Come on, it's me asking. What's up?"

She looks angry. "I was stood up, if you must know. Corey Matthews asked me on a date and never showed up. I really thought he liked me, Flynn. I feel like a fool because I, well…"

Flynn pulls her into his arms and my heart sinks when I see the murderous rage in his eyes. Great, now he'll head off for revenge on her behalf and we'll be in the shit again.

"Where's Winter?" I ask the only question that concerns me, and she sniffs.

"I don't know. The last I knew, she was in history. I haven't seen her since."

I glance at Malik, who looks worried, which isn't like him, and I feel the pressure building in my head. Nodding to Flynn to take Emma from the room, I say in a hushed voice, "What do you know?"

Malik shakes his head. "Not a lot, but I found this online." He holds up his phone and scrolls to a video on the internet. "It's one of those pay to view sites and it appears our Miss. English has another profession."

I watch our history teacher pleasuring herself on camera and feel sick. "That makes sense."

The sight of that fucking pink palace connects the dots. She's dressed like a schoolgirl and obviously earns way more money on her back than at her desk and I say urgently, "We need to find her."

Before we can, there's a loud knock on the door and Ivan races to open it and I hope to God it's my sister.

Instead, we see a distraught Miss. English shaking on the veranda with tears streaming down her face.

Ivan pulls her in and shoves her into a chair and I say roughly, "Where's Winter?"

"I don't know." Her frightened voice causes a pain in my heart because where the fuck is my sister?

"What happened?" Malik takes charge of the situation because he is always my calm voice of reason and she shakes, stuttering. "We went to town. I promised her a soda to cheer her up. She was so upset in class I wanted to help and thought that would get her to confide in me. We were nearly there when a car pulled in front of us, and I almost hit it. Three men got out and opened her door. I screamed, and she just laughed and told me that I'd played my part in getting her there and wouldn't be of any further use."

Nothing she says rings true and then she sobs, "They threatened me. Told me not to speak about this and deny anything happened. I'm to say I went to the restroom and found her gone and that if I value my life, I'll keep quiet. Winter changed before my eyes and told me she had planned this all along. She was getting out while she could and never going back. She arranged an escape months ago and to tell your father to go fuck himself."

I'm not sure how I'm still standing and one look at Alessandro confirms my worst fears. He looks worse than I do and Ivan growls, "You're a fucking liar."

He places his hand on her and she squeals in fright. "Please, you must believe me. The last thing she said was a message to you, Angelo."

"What message?" My voice is rough, and I almost can't speak as the pain sears my heart closed forever.

"She told me you have one night left and then your group will be torn apart forever."

The atmosphere darkens as we face our worst fear. First Winter and now it seems the rest of us. I refuse to think she's responsible for this. That's not my sister and I nod to

Ivan, who grasps Miss. English by the hair and pulls her before me. "You're lying." I hiss and nod to Malik.

He brings up the video of her online and she looks down as if in shame. "I'm not proud of that. It's the only way I can earn money. There's not enough pay being a teacher, and I want to save enough to buy myself a new life in a small town somewhere."

"Then tell us what you know, who you're working for, and where my sister is?" I am falling fast and need my friends to catch me because my sister can't have done this willingly. She wouldn't know how.

Miss. English sobs. "I'm so sorry, that's all I know. What shall I tell Principal Stoner?"

I nod to Ivan, who releases her, and she falls to the ground in a frightened heap. "You tell him nothing unless it's the truth. Now fuck off, you sick bitch, and go and play with yourself for money."

Ivan removes her and we hear a thud as she is tossed down the stairs outside and I am shaking so hard I don't know what to do. My sister. My beautiful, innocent sister is God only knows where and I don't have the faintest idea where to go from here.

The walls are closing in on me because I know what happens now. The End. It's the end for all of us because somehow that was a warning. We have one night to form our plans because tomorrow they're coming for us.

36

ANGELO

The house is in darkness and the only people who remain are five twisted souls and one very special guest.

Emma was moved back to her dorm, and she was happy to go when we explained our time at Rockwell was done. Flynn made up some story about Winter that satisfied her curiosity, and we have one night only to formulate the plan to find my sister and set us all free.

The candles burn all around and it looks like a fucking devil worship club, and we sit in a circle with our special guest and prepare to change our destinies.

I say in a voice devoid of any emotion.

"This is our final chance to agree on the plan. If you are in, you must sacrifice your heart."

All around me the solemn faces of my closest friends in the world stare at me with the dark look of the damned.

They each nod as I look at them in turn and when my gaze settles on Baron, he nods with a determination that settles any doubt I ever had of asking him.

He will be a worthy addition to our club because he has a power none of us understand. The man on the edge looking in and I know in my soul he will never let us down.

"Membership is painful. Do you understand the consequences of that?"

My voice is cold, emotionless and destroyed and one by one, they agree.

I nod to Flynn, who reaches behind him and as we all remove our shirts and toss them behind us, I take a deep breath.

"Then this begins. One by one, we sacrifice our hearts and join in blood as our commitment to Club Mafia. Malik, Angelo, Flynn, Ivan and Alessandro. Mafia. Baron sitting aside on the edge looking into the pit of hell."

I'm not sure if we can even go through with the commitment ceremony, but Flynn doesn't seem to have the same reservations and stares at the group with the mad eyes of a psychopath and grips his blade in his hand. Shaped like a claw, he rests it against his skin and growls, "I fucking pledge myself to this club against all others. My allegiance is to Club Mafia first and foremost and everything I do in life is for my brothers over my own family. *We are family now and to show my commitment, I sacrifice my heart.*"

The air is tense as he rests the blade against his skin and grins like a demented maniac. We watch as he presses the blade into his chest and laughs as the blood spills like the river of hell down his chest. He doesn't even flinch as he drags it down his skin, just above his heart and as his drops of blood spill onto the contract we will each sign with blood, it gives me my own strength to see this through.

Handing the contract to Ivan, who sits to his left, he

wipes the blade and hands it to our brother without even flinching.

The tattooed savage who is next in line utters the same words, read from the bloodied sheet and runs the blade down his own skin with all the aggression and the madness of hell. He roars as the blade slashes his skin and then grins as he signs his own name on the contract with his blood and then passes it to me.

All eyes focus on me as I steel myself and read the words on the page and make my own solemn vow. This club has to mean everything to its members because when you sell your soul to the devil, he keeps it forever. No matter what happens in the future, we work as a team bound by blood and common purpose.

We will leave tomorrow and become the enemy within, grabbing our empires from unsuspecting masters. As I repeat the same words, I just see my sister in my heart. Alone and afraid, set up for the cruellest of falls. I don't believe for a second that she betrayed us and whatever her reasons for leaving the way she did, they were done to protect every single one of us.

I slash the blade through my skin and drag three rivers of pain. My heart is clawed out and will never feel emotion again. There will be no tattoos with our club insignia. This needs a different level of commitment and as my blood joins my brothers, I am re-born an even bigger bastard than before.

Malik is next and his low voice slices through the silence as he pledges his heart and then Alessandro almost snatches the blade and slices his skin in one abrupt move. He growls the words and hands the blade to Baron, who studies it before reciting the same mantra spoken by every last one of us. As the final member pledges his blood, the candles burn with the hottest flames of hell. Souls united in damnation and God help anyone who gets in our way.

EXACTLY ONE HOUR LATER, our guests arrive, and we throw the biggest party Rockwell Academy has ever seen. We are out of control and don't care about the consequences of that because tomorrow we bid farewell to our freedom and fall in line.

Malik will return to Dubai and Ivan to Russia. Flynn heads to California and Alessandro to Boston. I'm heading to New York, where I will be the first to set our plan in motion. World domination the only way we know how. Power by marriage and our angels have been chosen already. Women who don't know what's in store for them and all selected for maximum effect. Married to mafia and sentenced to a life of sacrifice. No love, no affection and no shit because God can only help those women because they are the sacrifices needed to form an empire.

Club Mafia will combine the most powerful families in the land, all with one ultimate goal. Bringing down the men who made us in their image. Setting my sister free and taking control of our own lives.

This is it.

Let the games begin.

EPILOGUE

WINTER - ONE YEAR LATER

I am nervous for so many reasons I can't count them all. Today will be the hardest test that I cannot fail under any circumstances. Somehow, I have learned to shut away emotion this past year and focus on only one thing — survival.

Massimo sits like a burden wrapped around me, weighing me down and sucking any hope I have left. Like one of the fictitious Death Eaters, he is slowly sucking away any humanity within me and I will myself to get through today and make it back in one piece.

He holds my hand and gently plays with my fingers and sighs. "I like this color on you."

He studies the manicure he gave me last night, and then I watch him drop my hand and smooth out an imaginary crease in my black silk dress. "You must look perfect, my pet. I want to be the envy of everyone there. I have the brightest star in heaven, and she will shine so brilliant she will blind every person there tonight."

I feel his scrutiny and hope to God nothing is out of place, and he whispers, "Look at me, my pet."

Slowly, I turn and stare into eyes full of madness, although unlike Flynn, this man does not wear it well.

Just thinking of Flynn makes my soul weep and yet I push the image away just as quickly as it came and focus instead on my husband to get me through.

He frowns and says with a hint of steel in his voice, "Remember. I will hear everything you say. Pass this test, my pet, and you shall be rewarded. Fail and, well, we all know what happens then."

He laughs as if he's a fucking comedian and I nod, forcing a smile onto my lips. "I won't let you down, darling."

My heart thumps like a bass drum as I set my resolve in place. I can do this and I will do this because I have no other choice.

The moment we pull through the familiar gates, I almost doubt my own determination. The familiar becomes my nightmare as we join the long procession of cars making their way to the house.

If I feel anything, it's fear. Not for what's inside, but that I won't make it back. That is not an option, so I shut down inside as I have trained myself to do this past year—to survive.

The car sweeps to the front door and I hold my breath as we stop and Massimo steps out, tugging me with him.

His hand feels sweaty, and I know he is tense about this. I'm not sure why because we have more security than the Queen of England and I have seen first-hand how his organization operates.

Massimo Delauren is a feared mafia bastard for a very good reason. He has the biggest operation, the deadliest loyalty of his employees and hides behind a fortress. His dealings are legendary in the business and his punishments cruel and designed to invoke fear in the hearts of everyone who knows him. He is untouchable, and that is why I can't fail.

We walk hand in hand into my childhood home and the only thing that strikes me is how small it looks. Compared to Massimo's palace, this could fit into one small wing of it. He has several homes which are closely guarded like a fortress and all of them are equipped with a dungeon that he likes to visit frequently.

Pushing those images away, I follow him to a room filled with mourners and all eyes turn in our direction and a hush falls as we head inside. Not just because of him, either. Because of me, because today is the day I visit my family for the first time since I left.

My heart thumps as if it's afraid it won't make it, and Massimo grips my hand tightly and pulls me close by his side.

Then the moment arrives that I've been dreading and my brother steps away from the crowd and heads toward us, looking every inch the mafia don he has now inherited the title of.

"Massimo."

He addresses my husband first out of respect and Massimo says with a hint of steel in his voice, "Angelo, I am sorry for your loss."

My brother just nods, and I feel his piercing gaze searching me for answers that I am not prepared to give.

"Winter."

His deep familiar voice tests my resolve as Massimo knew it would and only the tightening on my fingers, crushing them in a warning, tells me my husband is as much on edge as I am.

"Please, follow me."

I nod because we knew this would be the first obstacle to overcome and as I walk beside my brother, I do so with my husband's hand firmly in mine.

We say nothing and as we reach the familiar room where my father ruled his empire, I wonder if I am really strong enough.

Massimo leans down and whispers, "I'll be waiting outside. Call me if you need me, my darling."

Then he leans down and brushes his lips against mine and I know it's purely for Angelo's attention and I nod, smiling up at him as if he's my fucking Prince Charming. "Thank you, my darling."

He gently strokes my face and looks at me with passion, and it always amazes me how well he plays this. Then again, he is very passionate about his favorite doll and so I smile as if he hung the moon and step inside the room.

The door closes behind us and when I see the coffin, all I feel is a surge of relief.

I walk across and peer inside and see my father looking as if he's sleeping peacefully. The cruel twist to his lips and the arrogant expression went with him to death, it seems.

Only the bullet hole square between his eyes tells me his ending was quick at least and I say bitterly, "Rot in hell, you bastard."

Angelo moves beside me and the urge to take his hand is overwhelming and I begin to shake inside. Trying to distract my thoughts, I say in an angry whisper, "It wasn't painful enough."

"It was my only chance, and all that matters is I killed

the miserable bastard as I always said I would."

The silence is ominous and for a moment we are fourteen again. Two souls joined for eternity, taking on the world.

Angelo moves closer and I move away from him. Creating distance between us in a powerful message to fuck off.

"Stay." Angelo's voice is firm and full of conviction, and I laugh derisively. "Why would I want to do that, Angelo?"

"Why wouldn't you?"

"Because I love my husband and I'm happy."

"Are you sure about that, Winter? You forget I know you better than anyone."

"You know nothing about me. When I left you that day, I was taken to Massimo. He has become my everything, and I realized how lucky I am. I fell in love, and we are happy. Why can't you accept that?"

He moves toward me, and I shrink back against the wall because God forbid he sees past my lies.

Grabbing my hand, he pulls me toward him and hisses, "Drop the act. We both know you don't mean one word of it. Tell me what he has over you. I'll set you free and I won't leave you to spend your days in hell with him."

Pushing him away, I say with a sneer. "Then you will ruin my life. You will make me unhappy because I'm telling the truth. I love my husband and he is everything to me. Why is that so hard to believe?"

I take a few deep breaths and say firmly, "The day I left, I told him everything. About your plans, and desire to ruin empires. In return for knowledge, he has given me everything. I sold you and your friends out for my own purposes and I would do it again in a heartbeat. You are all deluded if you think you can ever be greater than my husband, and so I am begging you to walk away. Leave me alone where I am happy because I don't want you. I don't *need* you, and the last thing I want is to ever see you again."

Taking a look at the open coffin, I spit into it, hitting my father's face in one direct hit. "Fuck you all. I hate you."

Turning, I make to leave and, in a flash, Angelo is by my side, pinning me against the wall and leaning in hisses, "When did you grow up into a bitch sister, this isn't you, trust me, I know. What hold does he have over you?"

"Love, Angelo. I love him, and why can't you accept that?"

I push him away, hoping like hell he hasn't creased my dress and smeared my red painted lips and with a deep breath I say coldly, "Enjoy your life, Angelo. I don't want to be part of it."

As I reach the door, I open it and Massimo steps forward and his eyes pass me as he looks into the room.

I'm not certain if he looks at the coffin or Angelo, but his deep voice scratches against my nerves as he says smoothly, "Death is so final, so peaceful really. Who knows what horrors went before the final act? Your father was a powerful man and yet even he never saw the ending coming for him. Unexpected, cruel and final."

His hand folds around mine and he says, "Have you paid your respects, my darling?"

"Yes, I have."

"Would you like to stay for a while and spend time with your brother?"

"No. I want to go home, my darling, where I belong."

He nods and I can't see the look he directs at my brother, but I'm pretty certain it's a triumphant one.

As I walk beside him, back the way we came, I just hope I've done enough.

We are back in the car inside ten minutes and as the door slams and the car moves away, Massimo laughs, which makes me relax—a little.

"Well done, my pet."

He reaches behind my ear and removes the listening device and tosses it to the floor.

"I knew you wouldn't let me down. I have trained my pet well, although I heard you curse, my darling. I am not happy about that."

A feeling of dread freezes my blood. Please God, no.

He fusses with my hair and smooths down my clothes, and smiles. "I am feeling generous and will overlook that for once. No, I am pleased with how today went and may allow you a few more excursions if you continue to please me. It feels good knowing your family is no longer a threat to us, so I will grant your wish."

"You mean…"

He smiles. "Tonight, you may have a sleepover."

The relief hits me inside and all the tension leaves me as I smile at him happily. "I can?"

He nods. "Please me, and I am very generous. I don't need to tell you what happens when you anger me, so all the time you do as expected, you will treated like a queen."

For the entire journey, I feel a lightness to my spirit that tells me I did the right thing, and I almost can't wait to get home.

As soon as we arrive at the most closely guarded fortress there is, I feel eager to get this over with.

Massimo laughs and pulls me with him toward his room and this is the side to him I prefer. Generous, kind even and caring and I just thank God I played my part so well.

We reach his room and I note the huge bed and silken sheets with not a crease in sight. The soft carpeting is new because at any hint of dirt, it is quickly ripped up and a fresh carpet laid. The freshly polished wood gleams and the mirrors sparkle and nothing is out of place because that is how *he* likes it.

He steps away from me and says almost as an aside.

"Follow me."

We head to the closet that could house a family of five and step inside a white painted mirage of everything a girl dreams of. Chandelier's sparkle and mirrors reflect the glass-covered shelves, with every item of clothing ever made it seems. Beautiful silks and taffeta. Cashmere and fur, all neatly arranged in order of color. Drawers of jewelry and impeccably placed rows of shoes, all individually lit under spotlights. This room is his dream and my nightmare and as he closes the door, he says with excitement lacing his voice.

"Take off your clothes."

I don't even think about it. I am so eager to please him and with care, I remove every item from my body, folding it up and placing it on the side where the maid will deal it with it later.

I move to the center of the room and stand on a kind of pedestal and feel the light warming my naked body while Massimo walks around me, admiring the view.

He runs his fingers against my flat stomach and then trails them across my breast. Then he frowns and sighs. "You have some growth; we need to deal with that."

I watch as he removes a razor from the drawer and carefully shaves away the stubble on every part of me and feeling the blade reminds me how close I am to pain and when he finishes, he steps back and looks at his handiwork critically.

Then he grabs some lotion and carefully massages every part of my body, and I will myself to stand as stiff as a statue. God, forbid I move or make a sound while he plays with his doll and I focus on only one thing. The sleepover.

He selects a beautiful silk nightgown and as he dresses me, the soft fabric falls down my body like a lover's embrace. I have the best that money can buy, so I'm the lucky one, I guess.

He drapes a matching silk robe around me and says with a great deal of satisfaction. "We need to tidy up that hair of yours."

Dutifully, I sit in the chair and wait patiently for him to comb out my long hair one hundred times and even the bite of the comb doesn't distract me from the happiness I'm feeling inside.

One final hurdle to jump and it will all have been worthwhile.

He drops low on the ground before me and runs his hand up my leg and then parts my thighs, lifting the nightdress with care as he kisses my skin and inhales the scent that he loves so much. Chanel. His favorite.

"You are so beautiful, my little pet. I always knew you would be. You have pleased me today and so tonight we both get what we want."

I say nothing and just paint a smile on my face as he sighs and covers my legs before reaching for my hand.

"Come. I am impatient to begin."

As I follow him back into his bedroom, I feel an excitement I rarely get to feel. I would do anything for this. I have sold my soul for this, and I follow him through the large living space to the door on the opposite side of his suite of rooms. He raises his finger, pressing his print to the biometric entry system to gain access and I hold it together for fear of anything spoiling this moment and as we step inside the room, my heart leaps and the emotion almost overcomes me until I push it away for later.

We approach the white crib set in the middle of the room and stand on either side of it looking in.

"There he is."

Massimo's soft voice spoils the moment, and fear sharpens my senses when he lifts my son into his arms.

"So beautiful, so small and so breakable."

He gently rocks him, and Frankie stirs from his sleep and cries a little. "Such a beautiful baby, just like his mother."

Massimo walks over to the window and my senses are on high alert as he gazes across the empire he runs.

"A blessing from God that we prayed for but never dared hope to see."

He laughs softly. "It was an ingenious plan but had an element of luck involved. Place you like forbidden fruit in the garden of Eden and hope temptation proved too much. Miss. English distracting your brother was her idea and I must say it worked a treat, but which one is the father, I wonder?"

I tense and plaster a blank look on my face and say in a voice devoid of emotion. "It could be any one of them."

He laughs and spins around and shakes his head. "So wanton, my little pet. So desperate to be loved. We knew it would only be a matter of time, and I had hoped our plan had worked. Not that it would have mattered if you came to me without this precious gift growing inside you. I had a suitable candidate lined up just in case."

He lifts my son high, and I am ready to pounce if necessary; a mother on the edge of insanity who would kill to protect her child.

"No, he is perfect regardless, because I now own the most valuable commodity there is. My son keeps you in line and my enemies away, because just the hint of a threat will force me to reveal my hand."

He strokes Frankie's head and leans down and kisses him gently. "You have our son for fourteen years, my darling, and then he's mine. I will leave you to enjoy the evening because I have a new toy waiting for me that I am keen to play with. Enjoy this generous gift because tomorrow it's business as usual."

As he walks toward me and hands me my son, I hold it together until he leaves, the door slamming behind me sealing me in a prison I never want to leave.

Clutching my son as tightly as possible, I let the dam burst and as the tears fall down my face, I whisper, "I love you Francesco and I will set us both free, I promise you that."

As he snuggles into my arms, I look at his beautiful face staring up at me and feel my heart tremble with emotion. So like his father. Dark hair and the darkest brown eyes with the longest lashes. My one night only is my most treasured memory and I will always have a reminder of what love feels like. I lied when I told Alessandro I was on the pill because I wanted to feel every part of him and never for one moment thought of the repercussions of that. It was the greatest decision I ever made because now I have purpose and love for the first time in my life. I know my reason for being here. I have my son and if I must sacrifice everything else I would do so in a heartbeat just to hold him in my arms and love him unconditionally.

I will bide my time and form my plan and when Massimo least expects it, I will kill the bastard and, unlike my father's death, it won't be quick. The murderous rage that swirls inside my heart is building, and I am counting down the hours until we are free.

THANK you for reading Club Mafia. This journey is just beginning and the next book in the series is Angelo's story.
The Boss
   Check it out here.

If you want to read **Baron's book**, just click on the link.

She ran from me.
I considered it a head start.
Watching her go was the purest form of betrayal.
She was always mine.
My wife in waiting.
But she decided her freedom was a better option — she was wrong.
She ran to a psychopath who tore her dreams to shreds.
At my request.
Then I took what was mine all along.
This time it was on my terms and our wedding has been arranged.

Tomorrow.
Then we return as husband and wife and there is nothing she can do about that.
The contract states, 'til Death Do Us Part.
But whose?
A dark romance with no cheating and hard-earned HEA

Thank you for reading this story.
If you have enjoyed the fantasy world of this novel, please would you be so kind as to leave a review on Amazon?

Join my closed Facebook Group

Stella's Sexy Readers

Follow me on Instagram

Carry on reading for more Reaper Romances, Mafia Romance & more.
Remember to grab your free copy of The Highest bidder by visiting stellaandrews.com.

ALSO BY STELLA ANDREWS

Dirty Hero (Snake & Bonnie)

Daddy's Girls (Ryder & Ashton)

Twisted (Sam & Kitty)

The Billion Dollar baby (Tyler & Sydney)

Bodyguard (Jet & Lucy)

Flash (Flash & Jennifer)

Country Girl (Tyson & Sunny)

The Romanos

The Throne of Pain (Lucian & Riley)

The Throne of Hate (Dante & Isabella)

The Throne of Fear (Romeo & Ivy)

Lorenzo's story is in Broken Beauty

Beauty Series

Breaking Beauty (Sebastian & Angel) *

Owning Beauty (Tobias & Anastasia)

Broken Beauty (Maverick & Sophia) *

Completing Beauty – The series

Five Kings

Catch a King (Sawyer & Millie) *

<u>Slade</u>

Steal a King

Break a King

Destroy a King

Marry a King

Baron

Standalone

The Highest Bidder (Logan & Samantha)

Rocked (Jax & Emily)

Brutally British

Deck the Boss

Reasons to sign up to my mailing list.

- A reminder that you can read my books FREE with Kindle Unlimited.
- Receive a monthly newsletter so you don't miss out on any special offers or new releases.
- Links to follow me on Amazon or social media to be kept up to date with new releases.
- Free books and bonus content.
- Opportunities to read my books before they are even released by joining my team.
- Sneak peeks at new material before anyone else.

stellaandrews.com

Follow me on Amazon

Printed in Great Britain
by Amazon